"Ryzard Vrbancic?" **she managed faintly. Please no.**

His gorgeous mouth twisted with ironic dismay. "As you can see. Who are you?"

Of course she could see. Now that Tiffany's brain was beginning to function, it was obvious this was the self-appointed president of Bregnovia. How did a name like Ryzard go from being something vaguely lethal to noble and dynamic simply by encountering the man in person? How had she not sensed or realized....

"There's been a mistake. I've made a mistake."

And yet her body responded to being in his presence. Even though she wasn't drunk and no music seduced her, her feet didn't want to move and her eyes kept being dragged back to his wide chest, where a sprinkle of hair had abraded her palms. His arms flexed as she watched, forcing her to remember being caught protectively against him when the fireworks had started and then being carried like a wilted Southern belle when sex had been the only thing on their minds.

Warily she eyed him. "I didn't know who you were last night."

"No?" His brow kicked up, dismissing her claim as a lie.

"No!"

"You sleep with strangers often?"

"Apparently you do, so don't judge me."

The 21st Century Gentleman's Club

Where the rich, powerful and passionate come to play!

For years there have been rumors of a secret society, where only the richest, the most powerful and the most decadent can embrace their every desire.

Nothing is forbidden in this private world of pleasure.

And when exclusivity is beyond notoriety, only those who are invited to join ever know its name....

Q Virtus

Now the truth behind the rumors is about to be revealed!

Find out in:

The Ultimate Playboy
by Maya Blake

July 2014

The Ultimate Seduction
by Dani Collins

August 2014

The Ultimate Revenge
by Victoria Parker

September 2014

Dani Collins

The Ultimate Seduction

 HARLEQUIN PRESENTS®

Recycling programs
for this product may
not exist in your area.

ISBN-13: 978-0-373-13270-6

THE ULTIMATE SEDUCTION

First North American Publication 2014

Copyright © 2014 by Dani Collins

This is a work of fiction. Names, characters, places and incidents are either the product of the author's imagination or are used fictitiously, and any resemblance to actual persons, living or dead, business establishments, events or locales is entirely coincidental.

This edition published by arrangement with Harlequin Books S.A.

For questions and comments about the quality of this book, please contact us at CustomerService@Harlequin.com.

Printed in U.S.A.

™ www.Harlequin.com

All about the author...
Dani Collins

DANI COLLINS discovered romance novels in high school and immediately wondered how a person trained and qualified for that amazing job. She married her high school sweetheart, which was a start, then spent two decades trying to find her fit in the wide world of romance writing, always coming back to Harlequin Presents®.

Two children later, with the first entering high school, she placed in Harlequin's Instant Seduction contest. It was the beginning of a fabulous journey toward finally getting that dream job.

When she's not in her Fortress of Literature, as her family calls her writing office, she works, chauffeurs children to extracurricular activities and gardens with more optimism than skill. Dani can be reached through her website at www.danicollins.com.

Other titles by Dani Collins available in ebook:

A DEBT PAID IN PASSION
MORE THAN A CONVENIENT MARRIAGE?
PROOF OF THEIR SIN
NO LONGER FORBIDDEN?

I've been lucky enough to work with a few different editors at Mills & Boon London. They're all made of awesome, but I must send a huge shout of appreciation to my current editor, Laurie Johnson. Not only has she made the transition into her care utterly painless, but this is our first book completely midwifed from start to finish by her. No spinal block required! Writer and book are happy and doing well. Thanks, Laurie!

CHAPTER ONE

TIFFANY DAVIS PRETENDED she wasn't affected by the hard stare her brother and father gave her when she entered her father's office. It wasn't easy to let people she loved pass judgment on whether she'd used sufficient concealer on her scars. Sometimes she wanted to throw the bottle of liquid beige into the trash and scream, *There. This is what I look like now. Live with it.*

But her brother had saved her life pulling her from the fiery car. He felt guilty enough for putting her in it. He still grieved for her groom, his best friend, and everything else Tiffany had lost. She didn't have to rub salt in his wounds.

Good girl, Tiff. Keep biting back what you really want to say. It's not like that got you into these skin grafts.

She came to a halt and sighed, thinking it was probably time for another visit to the head doctor if she was cooking up that sort of inner dialogue. But her harsh exhale caused both men to tense. Which made her want to rail all the louder.

Being angry all the time was a character shift for her. Even she had trouble dealing with it, so she shouldn't blame them for reacting like this. But it still fed her irritation.

"Yes?" She clicked her teeth into a tight smile, attempting to hold on to her slipping patience.

"You tell us. What's this?" Christian kept his arms folded as he nodded at the large box sitting open on their father's desk. The lid wore an international courier's logo, and the contents appeared to be a taxidermist's attempt to marry a raven to a peacock.

"The feather boa you asked for last Christmas?" Lame joke, sure, but neither man so much as blinked. They only stared at her as if they were prying her open.

"Be serious, Tiff," Christian said. "Why is the mask for you? Did you request to go in my place?"

A claustrophobic band tightened around her insides. A year in a mask had left her vowing to never feel such a thing on her face again. "I don't know what you're talking about."

The frost in her voice made both men's mouths purse. *Why did all of this have to be so hard?* The touchiness between her and her family was palpable every minute of every day. If she was short, they were defensive. If she was the least bit vulnerable, they became so overprotective she couldn't breathe.

They'd nearly lost her. She got that they loved her and were still worried about her. They wouldn't relax until she got back to normal, but she would never be normal again. It made the situation impossible.

"Where is it you think I want to go?" she asked in as steady a tone as she could manage.

"Q Virtus," her father said, as if that one word sufficed as explanation.

She shook her head and shrugged, still lost. Did they realize she was in the middle of an exchange worth five hundred million dollars? She didn't have much, but she did have a job now. Seeing as it involved running a multibillion-dollar company, she tried to do it well.

"Ryzard Vrbancic," Christian provided. "We put in a request to meet him."

Pieces fell together. *Q Virtus* was that men's club Paulie used to talk about. "You want to meet a puppet leader at one of those rave things? Why? The man's a despot."

"Bregnovia is asking for recognition at the UN. They're a democracy now."

She snorted in disbelief. "The whole world is ignoring the fact he stole the last dictator's money and bought himself a presidency? Okay."

"They're recovering from civil war. They need the sort of infrastructure Davis and Holbrook can provide."

"I'm sure they do. Why go the cloak-and-dagger route? Call him up and pitch our services."

"It's not that simple. Our country hasn't recognized his yet so we can't talk to him openly, but we want to be the first number on his list when recognition happens."

She rolled her eyes. Politics were so fun. "So you've set up this clandestine meeting—"

"It's not confirmed. That happens when you get there."

"That would be the broad 'you,' right? Like the universal 'they'?"

Christian's mouth tightened. He lifted out the feathery contents of the box. It was actually quite beautiful. A piece of art. The blend of blue-black and turquoise and gold feathers covered the upper eyes and forehead and—significantly—splayed down the left side in an eerily familiar pattern. Ribbons tailed off each side.

It was like looking in the mirror, seeing that reflection of her scar. A slithery feeling inside her torso made her heart speed up. She shook her head. She wasn't going anywhere, especially in public, with or without a crazy disguise.

"You understand how *Q Virtus* works?" her brother prodded. "This mask is your ticket in."

"Not *mine*."

"Yeah, Tiff, it is." He turned it around so she could see where her name was inscribed on the underside, along with *Isla de Margarita, Venezuela*. "See? Only you can attend."

His terse tone and shooting glance toward their father made it clear they'd spent some time pondering alternate solutions. Both men showed signs of deep frustration, a level of emotion usually reserved for when approval ratings were low. To see them so bent out of shape activated her don't-make-more-waves genes.

Your father is under a lot of pressure, dear. Do as he asks for now.

No, she reminded herself. She was living her life, not waiting for it to make everyone else's list of priorities. Still, she'd been raised to have civilized conversations, not be outright defiant. "I would think that taking off the mask to show your name defeats the purpose."

"There's a chip embedded. They know which mask belongs to which person, and as you can see, they only fit one face."

"They obviously know a lot about *me.* That's creepy. Doesn't it seem weird they would know how to cover my scars?"

"*Q Virtus* has an exceptional history of discretion and security," her father said, defending it with a kind of pompous grumpiness that surprised her. "Whatever they know about us, I'm sure it's kept very well protected."

A remarkably naive comment from a man who'd been in politics and business long enough to mistrust everyone and everything. Heck, he'd dragged her in here because he thought she'd undermined him with his brotherhood of secret handshakes, hadn't he?

"Dad, if you want to become a member—"

"I can't." He smoothed his tie, one of his tells when his ego was dented.

"Too old? Then Christian—?"

"No."

She was quite smart, had always had better marks than her brother, who fudged his way through just about everything, but she was missing something. "Well, Paulie was a member. What does it take?"

"Money. A lot of it. Paul Sr. was a member and once Paulie inherited, he had the means to pay the fee," her father said in a level tone.

Of course. Therein lay her father's envy and reverence. It must have eaten him alive that his best friend and rival for her mother's affections had possessed something he hadn't.

"When you were still in the hospital, I applied on your behalf, hoping to go as your proxy," Christian explained. "I didn't hear back until today." Glancing at their father, he added, "It is kind of creepy they know Tiff has finally recovered and taken over the reins of Davis and Holbrook."

"Everyone's talking about it. It's hardly a secret," her father dismissed with a fresh heaping of disapproval.

Tiffany bit back a sigh. She would not apologize for grappling her way into running the company now that she was well enough. What else would she do moving forward? Trophy wife and having a family was out of the question with this face.

Still, it was so *unladylike* to work, her mother reminded at every opportunity.

"I don't understand why they've accepted her. It's a men's club," her father muttered.

She eyed the mask, recalling the sorts of stories Paulie used to come home with after attending one of these *Q Virtus* things. "It's a booze-fueled sex orgy, isn't it?"

"It's a networking event," her father blustered.

Christian offered one of his offside grins. "It's a chance for the elite to let their hair down," he clarified. "But a lot of deals are closed over martinis and a handshake. It's the country club on a grander scale."

Right. She knew how that worked. Wives and daughters stood around in heels and pearls planning the Fourth of July picnic while husbands and fathers colluded to keep their money amongst themselves. Her engagement to Paulie, Jr. had been negotiated between the seventh and ninth holes of the top green, her wedding staged on the balcony by their mothers, her cake designed by the renowned chef, and all of it exploded into flames against the wrought-iron exit gate.

"This is all very interesting." It wasn't. Not at all. "But I'm in the middle of something. You'll have to sort this out yourselves."

"Tiffany."

Her father's stern tone was the one that made any good daughter spin, take a stance of dutifully planted feet, knees locked, hands knotted at her sides. She caught her tongue firmly between her teeth. "Yes?"

"Our friends in Congress are hoping for good relations with Bregnovia. I need those friends."

Because his hat was in the ring for the next election. Why was that always the only thing that mattered?

"I don't know what you expect me to do. Pitch our services while wearing a showgirl costume? Who would take that seriously? I can't go into a meeting without it, though. No one likes face-to-face interactions with this." She pointed at where her ear had been reconstructed and a cheekbone implant inserted.

Her father flinched and looked away, not denying that she was hard to look at. That hurt more than the months of screaming burn injuries.

"Maybe I could be your date," Christian said. "I don't know if members are allowed to bring an escort, but..."

"Bring my brother to the prom?" That certainly reinforced how far down the eligibility ladder she'd fallen. Her hands stayed curled at her sides, but mentally she cupped them around her tiny, shrunken heart, protecting it. *Love yourself, Tiff. No one else will.*

"Get me into the club and you won't have to leave your room until it's over," Chris said.

Hide the disfigured beast.

She had to close her eyes against her father's intense stare, the one that willed her to comply.

You weren't going to let yourself be a pawn anymore, she reminded herself.

"How long is this thing?" she heard herself ask, because what kind of family would she have, if not this one? Her friends had deserted her, and dating was completely off the table. Her life would be very dark and lonely if she alienated her parents and brother.

"We arrive at sunset on Friday night, and everyone is gone by Sunday evening. I'll make the travel arrangements," Christian said with quick relief.

"I wear this thing in *and* out. That's the deal, because I won't do this if I'm going to be stared at." Listen to her, talking so tough. She was actually scared to her toenails. What would people say if they saw her? She couldn't let it happen.

"As far as I know, everyone wears masks the whole time," Chris said, practically dancing, he was so elated.

"I'll be in my office," she muttered. *Searching for my spine.*

Ryzard Vrbancic abided by few rules beyond his own, but he left his newly purchased catamaran as the shadow of its mast stretched across the other boats in the Venezuelan marina. If he didn't climb the stairs before the red sky had inked purple, he would be locked out of the *Q Virtus* Quarterly.

Story of my life, he thought, but hoped that soon he'd be as welcome worldwide as the famous black credit card.

Security was its usual discreet step through a well-camouflaged metal detector that also read the chip in his mask. One of the red-gowned staff lifted her head from her tablet as he arrived and smiled. "We're pleased to see you again, Raptor. May I escort you to your room?"

She was a pretty thing, but the *petite q's* were off-limits, which was a pity. He hadn't had time to find himself a lover for weeks. The last had complained he spent more time working than with her, which was apparent from her spa and shopping bills. They were as high as his sexual frustration.

His situation should improve now, but he'd have to be patient a little longer. Like the music that set a vacation tone, the *petite q's* provided atmosphere. They could stroke an ego, dangle off an arm, flirt and indulge almost any reasonable request, but if they wanted to keep their job, they stayed out of the members' beds. Being smart and career minded along with attractive and engaging, the *petite q's* tended to side with keeping their jobs.

Such a pity.

His current escort set up his thumbprint for the door then stepped inside his suite for his briefing. "You have a meeting request from Steel Butterfly. Shall I confirm?"

"A woman?" he asked.

"I don't have the gender of our clients, sir."

And if she did know, she wouldn't say, either.

"No other requests?" He was hoping for a signal from international bodies that his petition to the UN was receiving a nod.

"Not at this time. Did you have any?"

Damn. He'd come here knowing he had a meeting request, hoping it would be a tip of the hand on his situation. Now he was under lockdown and liable to be taking a sales pitch of some kind.

"Not at present. I'll accept an introduction on that one, nothing longer." He nodded at her tablet.

"The time and location will be transmitted to your smartwatch. Please let us know if I can arrange anything else to ensure your satisfaction while you're with us."

He followed her out, confident that everything he'd preordered was in the suite. Zeus was exceptionally good at what he did. Ryzard had never had an issue of any kind while at *Q Virtus,* which made the exorbitant membership fee and elaborate travel and security arrangements worth the trouble.

Entering the pub-style reception lounge, he saw roughly thirty people, mostly men in tuxedos and masks. They stood with a handful of gorgeous *petite q's* wearing the customary red designer gowns.

He accepted the house drink for this session, rum over ice with a squeeze of lime and a sugared rim, then glanced at his watch. At his four o'clock, a collection of dots informed him the small conclave of men to his right included Steel Butterfly.

He had no idea where Zeus came up with these ridiculous nicknames, but he supposed Raptor was apt for him, coming from the Latin meaning to seize or take by force. The bones of several dinosaurs in that category had been uncovered in his homeland of Bregnovia, too.

Eyeing the group, he wondered which one was his contact. One accepted a drink from a *petit q* and handed her his watch. It didn't matter, he decided. He wasn't interested in beginning a conversation in public that he was scheduled to have in private tomorrow. He waited until he was out of range in the gambling hall to activate his identity on his own watch. This resulted in an immediate invitation to join the blackjack table.

He sat so he could read the screen mounted near the ceiling in the corner. It subtly manifested and dissolved with blurbs on presentations and entertainment to be held over the course of the *Q Virtus* Quarterly. Tastemakers, trendsetters and thought leaders were flown in to provide rich, powerful, political forces such as himself with the absolute cutting-edge information and samples of global economics and technology. Meanwhile, at tables such as this one, he would pick up the other side of the coin: gossip about a royal's addiction, a cover-up of a coup attempt on a head of state, a lie that would be accepted as truth to stem international panic.

He could only imagine what was said about him, but he didn't let himself dwell on what was likely disapproval and distrust. His people were free, his country independent. That was the important thing.

Still, thoughts of what it had cost him crept in, threatening to inject disappointment and guilt into an otherwise pleasant if staid evening. He folded his hand, left the table and lifted a rum off a passing waiter's tray as he moved outside in search of entertainment.

CHAPTER TWO

TIFFANY WAS STUCK and it was a sickeningly familiar situation, the kind she'd sworn she'd never wind up in again.

She'd love to blame Christian. He had urged her to step through the door when he'd been refused entry. *Go in and ask,* he'd hissed, annoyed.

Since her worst nightmare these days was being stared at, she'd forgone arguing on the stoop and stepped through the entranceway. Inside, pixies in designer nightgowns had fawned over the arriving men in masks. She'd looked around for a bell desk, and a stud named Julio had come forward to introduce himself as a *petite q.*

She, a seasoned socialite, had become tongue-tied over the strapping young man in a red footman's uniform. It was more than two years since she'd been widowed on her wedding day. Even without the scars, that would be bad mojo. Men didn't call, didn't ask her out. If she was in a room with a live one, they rarely looked her in the eye, always averting their gaze. She didn't exist for them as a potential mate.

Julio didn't attract her so much as astonish her. He didn't know what lurked beneath the mask and was all solicitous manners as he offered his services. "I see this is your first visit with us," he said after a brief glance at his tablet. "Please allow me to orient you."

She was completely out of practice with his type—the valet who never overstepped his station, but still managed to convey that he appreciated being in the presence of beauty. She'd haltingly fielded his questions about whether her travel had been pleasant as he smoothly escorted her into an elevator.

When he asked if she had any specific needs he could attend to while she was here, she'd come back to reality. "My brother needs a hall pass, or a mask. Whatever. Can you make that happen?"

"I'll send the request to Zeus, but the doors will be closing in a few minutes. Once we're in lockdown, no one comes or goes. Unless it's an emergency, of course." He'd lifted his head from tapping his tablet.

Lockdown? Alarmed, she'd tried to text Christian only to be informed that external service was cut off while inside the club.

"Cell phones and other cameras are discouraged, as is the sending of photos outside the club. Security will locate him and communicate his options," Julio assured her, then explained that if her requested meeting was accepted, the time and location would be sent to her Inspector Gadget watch.

"Where *are* we? A hollowed-out volcano?" she asked as he set up her thumbprint entry to her room.

"No, but we're working on obtaining one," he said, deadpan. "Now, you'll want to wear your watch throughout your stay. It tells a lot more than time. May I show you?"

Hearing that her scheduled meeting with the Bregnovian dictator wasn't a sure thing was a relief. Her father would be furious if she didn't go in Christian's place, but if the request was rejected, she would be off the hook. Still, she hoped her brother would be granted entry and save her worrying about any of it. She pressed Julio out of her suite with instructions to inform her about Christian as soon as possible.

Her suite was enough of an oasis to calm her nerves. Her

privileged upbringing had exposed her to some seriously nice digs, but she had to admit this was above and beyond. No expense had been spared on the gold fixtures, original art or silk bedding. The new clothes in the wardrobe were a pleasant distraction. Christian had said something about samples of prototypes being handed out to members. *If you don't want them, I do.*

She supposed he was referring to the spy watch Julio had shown her, but she was more interested in the designer gowns. Discreet labels informed her they were from the best of the best throughout South America, all in stunning colors and fabrics. Several were off-the-shoulder, figure-enhancing styles that would cover her scars.

Interesting.

Not that she had anywhere to wear them. She didn't intend to leave her room, but she would make the most of the in-suite amenities, she decided. Call it a vacation from her family. She'd work in peace for a few days.

Work, however, was next to impossible without Wi-Fi service to the external world, and besides, a calypso band was calling to her from below her open French doors. She *loved* dancing.

Full darkness had fallen, so she sidled into the shadows behind a potted fern on her balcony and gazed longingly at the party below, feeling rather like Audrey Hepburn in that old black-and-white. It was such a world beyond her. The pool's glow lit up ice sculptures on the buffet tables. Bartenders juggled open bottles, putting on a cocktail show as they poured fast and free while women in red gowns cha-cha'd with men in tuxedos and masks.

This whole mask thing was weird. As they'd flown south in the company jet, Christian had explained it allowed the world's elite to rub shoulders in a discreet way. Sometimes it was best for the biggest players to take their meetings in secret, so as not to cause speculative dips in the stock exchange. Certain celebrities stole these few days to relax without interruption by fans. *Q Virtus* catered to whatever the obscenely rich needed.

I need a new face, she thought sourly, but even the cavernous pockets her husband had left her weren't deep enough to buy a miracle.

She looked to where she'd left her mask dangling off a chair back's spire.

Despite her anxiety with the abrupt change of plans when she arrived, she had felt blessedly anonymous behind her mask as she had walked through the lobby and halls to her room. It had been an extraordinary experience to feel normal again. No one had stared. She had looked exactly like everyone else.

Hmm. That meant she didn't have to stay here like Rapunzel, trapped in the tower with the real world three stories below and out of her reach.

With her heart tripping somewhere between excitement and trepidation, she fingered through the gowns hanging in the wardrobe. The silk crepe in Caribbean blue would expose her good right leg, but not so high as to reveal where her grafts had been taken. After months of physiotherapy, she'd moved back into her old workout routine of yoga, weights and treadmill. She possessed all of her mother's vanity along with the genetic jackpot in the figure department. Only family saw her these days, and she hardly dressed to impress, but she was actually very fit.

Alone in the suite, she held the gown up to her body, then, without her mother there to discourage her, dared to try it on.

Whoever this Zeus guy was, he sure knew how to dress a woman. Especially one with defects to hide. The single sleeve went past her wrist in a point that ended in a loop of thread that hooked over her middle finger. The bodice clung to her waist and torso, plumping breasts that remained two of her best original features. She had to give her backside the credit it deserved, too. When she buckled on new shoes that were little more than sky-high heels and a pair of saucy blue-green straps, it was like being hugged by old friends. She almost wept.

Filtering her image through her lashes as she looked in the mirror, she saw her old self. *Hi, Tiff. It's nice to see you again. 'Bout time, too.*

Makeup didn't completely cover her scars, nothing could, but she enjoyed going through her old ritual after using the concealer, taking her time to layer on shadow and liner, girling herself up to the max. By the time she was rolling spirals into her strawberry blond hair, she was so lost in the good ol' days, she caught herself thinking, *I wonder what Paulie will say.*

The curling iron tagged her cheek where she would never feel it, and she nearly broke down. *You're not Cinderella, anymore, remember? You're the ugly stepsister.*

No. Not tonight. Not when she felt confident and beautiful for the first time since her wedding day. Had she been happy then? She couldn't remember.

Don't go there.

Gathering the top half of her hair over her crown, she tied the mask into place, then let her loose curls fall to hide the strap that circled her skull. Oddly, the mask wasn't as traumatic to wear as she'd feared. It didn't suction onto her face and make her feel trapped in a body that writhed in agony. It stood cocked like a fascinator to cover the left side of her face, while the feathers arranged around her eyes gave an impression of overly long lashes that layered backward to cover her forehead and hairline. She had expected it to be heavy, but it was as light as, well, feathers. They tickled the edges of her scars, where her skin was extra sensitive, making her feel feminine and pretty.

Staring at herself in the full-length mirror, she allowed

that she *was* pretty. After painting on a coat of coral lipstick, she did a slow twirl and caught herself grinning. Smiling felt odd, as if she was using muscles that had atrophied.

She lifted the weighty watch on her wrist, the one that identified her as Steel Butterfly. More like a broken one. Her sides didn't even match.

It didn't have to make sense, she assured herself as she tossed her lipstick into her pocketbook then realized she didn't need either room key or credit card. Such freedom! For a few hours, she would be completely without baggage.

Taking nothing but lighthearted steps, she left to join the party.

Ryzard could drink with the best of them. He'd spent the older half of his childhood in Munich, had managed vineyards in France and Italy, and had lived in parts of Russia where not finishing a bottle of vodka was a gross insult to the host. He was restless enough to get legless tonight, but so far he'd consumed only enough to become mellow and hungry. The cashmere breeze and the scents of beach and pineapple and roasting pig aroused his appetite—all his appetites. He'd mentally stripped the nearest *petite q's* and was considering a pass at one of the female members currently being scouted by every other bachelor here—along with some of the married members.

Not Narciso, aka the Warlock of Wall Street, though. He chatted with his friend long enough to see the man wasn't just here with his wife, but besotted by her. Lucky bastard. Ryzard countered his envy by reminding himself that love was a double-edged sword. He wouldn't ruin his friend's happiness by saying so, but he had once looked forward to marital bliss. Luiza had died before they found it, and the anguish was indescribable. No matter how pleased he was for his friend, he would never risk that toll again.

He'd stick to the less permanent associations one found, enjoyed and left at parties such as this one.

Glass panels had been fitted over the lap pool, turning it into a dance floor that glimmered beams of colored light beneath the bouncing feet. People were having a lively time, keeping the band's quick salsa beat rapping. The drummer stared off to the left, however, his grin male and captivated.

Ryzard followed the man's gaze and his entire being crackled to attention.

Well beyond the pool's light, in a corner mostly blocked by a buffet table and ice sculpture, a woman undulated like a cobra, utterly fascinating in her hypnotic movements timed perfectly with the music. Her splayed hands slid down her body with sexy knowledge, her hips popped in time to the beat, and her feet kick-stepped into motion.

She twirled. The motion lifted her brassy curls like a skirt before she planted her feet wide and swayed her weight between them. The flex of her spine gave way to a roll of her hips, and she was back into motion again.

Setting down his drink, Ryzard beelined toward her. He couldn't tell if the woman had a partner, but it didn't matter. He was cutting in.

She was alone, lifting her arms to gather her hair, eyes closed as she felt the music as much as heard it. She arched and stretched—

He caught her around the waist and used the shocked press of her hands at his shoulders to push her into accepting his lead, stepping into her space, then retreating, bringing her with him. As he moved her into a side step, she recovered, matching his move while her gaze pinned to his.

He couldn't tell what color her eyes were. The light was too low, her feathery mask shadowing her gaze into twin glinting lights, but he reacted to the fixation in them. She was deciding whether to accept him.

A rush of excitement for the challenge ran through him.

After a few more quick steps, he swung her into half pivots, catching each of her wrists in turn, one bare, one clad in silk, enjoying the flash of her bare knee through the slit of her skirt.

How had she been overlooked by every man here? She was exquisite.

Lifting her hand over her head, he spun her around then clasped her shoulder blades into his chest. Her buttocks—fine, firm, round globes as if heaven had sent him a valentine—pressed into his lap. Bending her before him, he buried his nose in her hair and inhaled, then followed her push to straighten and matched the sway of her hips with his own.

Tiffany's heart pounded so hard she thought it would escape her chest. One second she'd been slightly drunk, lost in the joy of letting the salsa rhythm control her muscles. Now a stranger was doing it. And doing it well. He pulled her around into a waltz stance that he quickly shifted so they grazed each other's sides, left, right, left.

She kicked each time, surprised how easily the movements came back to her. It had been years, but this man knew what he was doing, sliding her slowly behind his back, then catching her hand on the other side. He pushed her to back up a step, bringing one of her arms behind his head, the other behind her own. A few backward steps and they were connected by only one hand, arms outstretched, then he spun her back into him, catching her into his chest.

He stopped.

The conga beat pulsed through her as he ran his hands down her sides. Her own flew to cover his knuckles, but she didn't stop him. It felt too amazing. His fingertips grazed the sides of her breasts, flexed into the taut muscles of her waist and clasped her hips to push them in a hula circle that he followed with his own, his crotch pressed tight to her buttocks.

Sensual pleasure electrified her. No one touched her anymore. After being a genderless automaton for so long, she was a woman again, alive, capable of captivating and enticing a man. She nudged her hips into his, flashing a glance back at him.

He narrowed his eyes and held her in place for one deliberate thrust before he spun her into the dance, their energetic quick steps becoming an excuse to look at each other as he let her move to the farthest reach of his hand on hers.

She had been a bit of a tease in her day, secure in the knowledge everyone knew she was engaged. She'd been able to flirt without consequence, enjoying male attention without feeling threatened by it. This stranger's undisguised admiration was rain on her desert wasteland of feminine confidence. Climbing her free hand between her breasts to the back of her neck, she thrust out her chest then let the music snake up and down her spine as she flexed her figure for his visual pleasure.

His feral show of teeth encouraged her while his sheer male sexiness called to the woman in her, urging her to keep the notice of such a fine specimen. He might have started out his evening in a tux, but at some point he'd stripped down to the pants and the shirt, which was open at the collar and rolled back to his forearms at the sleeves. The mask he wore was vaguely piratical in its black with gold trim and wings at his temple, but the nose piece bent in a point off the end of his nose, suggesting a bird of prey.

A hunter.

And she was the hunted.

Her heart raced, excited by the prospect of being pursued. She wanted to be wanted.

Splaying her feet, she allowed her knees to loosen. The slit of her skirt parted to reveal her leg, and she made the most of it, watching him as she rolled her hips in a figure eight, showing off her body, enticing him with a come-hither groove.

He planted a foot between hers, surrounding her without touching her, hands raised as if he was absorbing energy from her aura. The sultry tropical air held an undertone of spicy cologne and musky man. Reaching out, she shaped the balls of his hard shoulders with her hands and climbed them to the sides of his damp neck, sidling close so they sidestepped back and forth, swaying together in time to the music, bodies brushing.

His wide hands flattened on her shoulder blades and slid with deliberation to the small of her back then took possession of her hips. As his unabashed gaze held hers, he pulled her in to feel the firm ridge of his erection behind his fly.

A flood of desire, not the trickles of interest she'd felt in the past, but a serious deluge of passion, transformed her limbs into heavy weights and flooded her belly with a pool of sexy heat. She became intensely aware of her erogenous zones. Her breasts ached and her nipples tingled into sharp, stinging points. Between her thighs, her loins pulsed with a swollen, oversensitive need.

As if he knew, he shifted and his hard thigh pressed into her vulnerable flesh. She gasped and her neck weakened as he bent over her. She dropped her head back and he followed, taking her body weight on his thigh. His nose grazed her chin, then her collarbone. His lips hovered between her breasts. Slowly he brought her up again and leaned his mouth close enough to tease her parted lips.

He was a stranger, she reminded herself, but her lips felt swollen and she desperately wanted the pressure of his mouth—

A clap of thunder exploded in the sky.

Jolted, she found herself smothered against his chest, his hard arms tight around her, one hand shielding the back of her head, fingers digging in with tension. Her mask skewed, cutting into her temple. Beneath her cheekbone, his heart slammed with power.

The claps and squeals and whistles continued and his arms relaxed enough she could fix her mask and look up. Fireworks painted the starscape in flowers and streaks of red and blue and green that dissolved into sparkles of silver and palms of gold.

As people moved into their space, he steered her away from the crowd, into a corner around a partition where they were hidden in an alcove. She set her hands on the concrete rampart and leaned back into the living wall he made behind her, eyes dazzled by the bursts of color reflected on the water as the fireworks continued to explode before and above them. The band switched to an orchestrated classic that matched the explosions, filling her with awe and visceral excitement.

Already fixed in the moment, they became one being, she and this stranger, their bodies pressed tight as they watched the pyrotechnics. His hands moved over her, absently at first, shaping her to his front. She responded, encouraging his touch by rubbing her buttocks into the proof that she could still arouse a man. When his hands cupped her breasts, bold and knowledgeable, she linked her own hands behind his neck, arching into his touch, reveling in the pressure of his palms and the thumbing of her nipples.

Dropping her head to the side, she turned her face and lifted her mouth, inviting his kiss with parted lips. He bent without hesitation, nothing tentative in the way he captured her mouth. Thorough and unhurried, he continued to caress her as he took sumptuous possession of her lips.

She ran her fingers into his hair, greeting his tongue with her own, inhibition melted by pure desire. Distantly she was aware this was out of character, but she wasn't Tiffany. Not the Tiffany of today and not the old one, either. Tonight she was the woman she wished she could have been. She was every woman. Pure woman.

Tonight she had no man to think about but this one. She didn't care that she didn't know him. She and Paulie hadn't known each other, either, not really, not the way a husband and wife should. Not in the biblical sense. She hadn't slept with him or any man.

But she wanted to. She had ached for years to experience sexual intimacy.

A strong male hand stroked down her abdomen and skimmed off to the top of her thigh, making her mewl in disappointment. Then he fingered beneath the slit of her skirt and she had to pull away from his kiss to draw in a gasp as he followed bare skin into the sensitive flesh at the top of her leg.

She stilled.

His arm across her torso tensed and the hand on her breast hesitated briefly before he continued caressing her, lightly and persuasively, both hands teasing her with the promise of continued pleasure.

A moan of craving left her and she shuddered in acceptance.

A streak of light shot skyward and his touch moved into her center, exploring satin and lace that were damp with anticipation. She couldn't help covering his hand with her own, pinning his touch where she ached for pressure.

He seemed to know what she needed more than she did. As he fondled her, her eyes drifted closed and her head fell back to rest against his shoulder. She bit her lip, ripples of delight dancing through her. Was she really doing this? Rubbing her behind into his erection, not caring they were in public, that she didn't know him, that this was all about her pleasure?

He started to draw his hand away and she turned her face to the side, a cry of disappointment escaping her, but he was only hooking her panties down her hip and returning to trace and part and seek and find.

She released a moan of pure joy.

He caught her chin in his other hand and tilted her face up for his kiss while his touch on her mound became deliberate and intimate and determined.

She let it happen. She held very still and kissed him back with naked passion, aware of the light breeze caressing where she was exposed to the shadows of the rampart and the velvety night air. She let him stroke her into delirious intensity, her awareness dimmed at the edges so she was focused on the pleasure he was delivering, plucking and teasing and bringing her closer.

Over the water, the biggest rockets exploded like thunder, sending shock waves through her that made her quiver in stunned reaction. The reverberations echoed inside her, sparking where he stroked, sending a wild release upward and out to the ends of her limbs. He pinched her nipple, and like a flashpoint, she was blind to everything but white light and astonishing pleasure. Glorious waves of joy crashed in, submerging her in tumultuous ripples that he seemed to control, pressing one after another through her with the rub of his fingertip.

As the fireworks dimmed to puffs of smoke surrounding a barge in the bay, her climax receded, leaving her a puddle of lassitude in his steely arms.

He adjusted her panties and started to turn her. She obeyed the command in his hands, wanting to kiss him, to thank him—

Without a word, he drew her across the balcony to a set of shallow stairs leading to the beach. She wobbled, partly because her legs were wet noodles, partly because her heels couldn't find solid purchase in the sand. He scooped her up, carrying her along with easy strength into a cabana encircled by heavy curtains.

Inside he set her on her feet and steadied her with one hand while he raked the cloth door closed behind them. Without a word, he scraped the mask off his face and yanked his shirt open, peeling it off his shoulders and throwing it aside.

She couldn't see his face, not really. It was barely a shade above pitch-black in here, but the glow of satin skin increased as he toed off his shoes and opened his fly, stripping without ceremony.

Sweet Lord, what a man. He stepped closer and she couldn't help reaching out to test the flat muscles of his abdomen, learning them by feel more than sight. Hot and damp, he reacted to her touch with a tense of muscles and a muffled curse, making her smile in the dark, pleased she had an effect on him.

Her hand bumped into his. He was applying a condom.

Curious, she lightly explored his latex-covered shape. As she did, the pressure of her mask shifted.

She knocked his touch away before she thought about what she was doing.

Stillness came over him.

She tried to penetrate the dark and read his face—which was what he was likely doing. He probably thought she was having second thoughts.

Hell, no. She might never have another chance to lose her virginity. Not like this, so caught up in desire she was shaking with it.

"Leave it on," she whispered.

His hands lowered to her shoulders, one skimming down the edge of her bodice under her arm. She knew what she was looking for.

"That, too." Catching his hand away from her zipper, she drew him toward the bed.

In the same way he'd taken her over on the dance floor, he took the lead. A tip of his weight, a knee in the bed and she was lifted and placed half under him in one smooth motion. Her startled exhale clouded between them as a hand sought beneath her skirt, catching at her panties then pausing.

She couldn't help chuckling, understanding the implicit question. Lifting her hips, she invited him to strip them off her. They caught on her shoe, and neither of them bothered to finish the job.

He hitched her skirt then tucked her neatly under him, his legs moving with practiced ease to part her knees wide.

More surprised than shocked, she stilled, bracing herself, wanting this, but not as lost in the moment as she'd been. That was okay. She'd had her fun and she wanted to remember everything about this encounter. Cataloguing the flex of his shoulders under the stroke of her hands, the weight of his hips, the roughened texture of his legs on her smooth inner thighs, she waited.

He teased her, rubbing the head of his erection against her and reawakening her senses. As she hummed a response, he kissed her, deeply, dragging her back into the well of desire she thought she'd left outside on the ramparts.

Sliding her knee up to his hip, she hooked her calf over his buttock and quite suddenly, it was happening. His flesh was pressing for entrance, stretching her. Oh, wow. It hurt, but not bad. She'd experienced pain way worse than this, but it was still very intimate. She bit her lip and concentrated on accepting him, breathing through the sting and countering her instinctive tension—

He swore and the hand in her hair tightened enough to pull, even though she suspected it wasn't intentional. His big body shook with tension.

"I'm hurting you," he said in a voice so gruff she couldn't discern what kind of accent he had.

"It's okay. It feels good. I like it." This was so primeval. Drinking in his scent, she licked his neck, wanting this delicious, mysterious man imprinted on her for all time.

Arching, she discovered there was more of him to take. Squeezing her leg to encourage him, she met resistance. Rather than press into her, he kissed her again, using his tongue, and lifted enough to sidle a hand between them, caressing where they joined. In moments he had her twisting in excitement, and a second later, he slid deep into her.

Ah, *this* was what it was all about.

Eyes wide open to the dark cabana, she hugged his rugged body and learned the dip in his spine and the shape of his buttocks. His tense muscles flexed as he retreated from her depths, pulling strings of sensations through her: echoes of sting, loss, but delicious friction, too. He smoothly filled her again, his big body trembling with strain as he controlled his movements. The smart was still there, but the pleasure was incredible.

Purring, she lifted her hips to his, clasping him with her inner muscles, kissing him with extravagant joy, telling him she loved everything he was doing to her.

For a second, he let her feel his full weight, the full power of his muscles as he caged her beneath him and pressed a hard, hungry kiss on her. The fingers tangled in her hair pulled again, and he held himself in stark possession of her. She could swear she felt him pulsing deep inside her.

Then his fingers massaged her scalp in gentle apology and he lifted slightly, withdrew and slowly began to thrust again. The music dimly entered her consciousness from far away as they danced, him leading her through the erotic steps as he lowered her zip and exposed her breast to his hand and mouth.

She sang breathy notes of acute pleasure and sensual agony, wanting this twisting, exciting play to go on for the rest of her life. But everything he did made the sweet pleasure intensify. Their lovemaking grew better and better, driving her up the scale of passion to exquisite heights. When he ran his hand up the bare thigh that bracketed his hip, and branded her buttock with his palm, lifting her into his quickening thrusts, she moaned in approval, needing that faster pace, that wild stimulation.

Climax arrived suddenly and more powerfully than the first. She clawed at him, stunned by the release, fixated by the intense sensation of his fullness inside her while she orgasmed. He cried out raggedly and shuddered over her and within her, pushing to take deep possession of her, holding them both on that place of ecstatic perfection.

Suffused with bliss, she didn't move afterward, just waited for her heart to slow and listened as his breath settled. In the distance, the music continued and voices rose in conversation and laughter.

At the first shift of his body to relax and leave hers, the first easing of his implacable lock of his hips against hers, she dropped her hands and removed her leg from his waist. Her long history with bandage changes gave her the knowledge that quick and ruthless was best, even though it hurt like hell.

He surprised her by merely shifting his weight off her a little before he pressed a kiss to the corner of her mouth then nuzzled his lips down her bare cheek to her ear. "That was incredible. Thank you."

She couldn't help the smile that grew unseen in the dark, or the way she warmed with pride and eye-stinging gratitude. "Thank *you*. I didn't expect anything like this to happen tonight," she confessed, even though she could hear the delight in her voice. He thought she was *incredible*.

"I'm pleased I could make your first time memorable."

Her heart stopped. "You could tell it's my first time?" She felt like the most gauche girl alive.

"I come to all of these. I know the regulars, and I've

never seen you before. I would have remembered," he added with another buss of warm lips against her cheekbone.

Oh, God, *that's* what he meant. She swallowed her relieved laughter, then stiffened as voices approached their cabana.

"We should go somewhere more private." He gently lifted off her, chivalrously flicking her skirt to cover her as he rolled away.

Everything in her protested, but she sat up on the other side of the narrow bed. As she tucked her breast back into her dress and closed the zipper, his hand curled around her upper arm, hot and commanding, drawing her into tipping back against him.

"I'm on the top floor. Are you closer?"

"I can't," she whispered with genuine regret, senses distracted by the musky scent surrounding him and the damp heat of his chest so close to her nose. She tilted her face to find his lips in a soft kiss of reluctant goodbye.

He didn't move his lips against hers except to say, "Why not?"

"It's complicated. I shouldn't have come out at all." Their breaths mingled. "I hope you *will* remember me," she admitted, feeling safe to reveal the bald longing here in the anonymous dark.

"I'll always wonder why, won't I?" he said with edgy dismay.

"And then you'll remember I wanted to keep this unspoiled by real life."

This time when she pressed her mouth to his, he kissed her back. Hard and thorough, so her heart rate picked up and her arms wanted to snake around his neck.

She wasn't about to hang around until the lights came on, though. She didn't want to see his face when he saw hers.

Pulling away, she stood and shook out her skirt, stepped her underwear off her heel and left them on the mat. Quite the cheeky Cinderella move. Her mother would never quit the slut-shaming if she knew.

Tiffany felt no guilt, however, no shame and no embarrassment as she slipped out of the cabana and up the stairs, past the pool and its raging party, toward the elevators and back to her room. Only sensual satisfaction and poignant *what-ifs* followed her steps.

CHAPTER THREE

RYZARD'S WATCH GAVE a muted beep, reminding him he had a meeting in ten minutes.

Annoyed, he rose from the small table where he'd sat for the last thirty minutes eating a meal he would have preferred to have taken in his room. He swept the breakfast room once more for a certain woman in a mask that made him think of a falcon's smoothly feathered head. A woman who was both gloriously uninhibited, yet had been so tight, he had feared as he entered her that she would call a halt.

A light sweat broke over him as he recalled possessing her, never having felt so—

He cut short the thought, stung by a dart of shame that he was on the verge of elevating a meaningless hookup past the only woman he would ever love. There was no comparison. Forget it all.

Good thing he hadn't allowed the *petite q* to send a message on his behalf. He'd been tempted, but the tight security here did him a favor, preventing him from a weak moment. All he'd had was a description of her mask, but when he had inquired to the nearest *petite q,* she had assured him she could deliver an invitation to the mysterious woman to join him at breakfast. She couldn't, however, divulge the member's name or moniker.

He'd declined, not wanting to look desperate. Not wanting to feel so desperate, but after the blood-chilling thought

he'd just had, he *didn't* wish to see her again. Their somewhat literal bumping of two strangers in the night was
nothing significant. A letting off of steam. If it had seemed
particularly intense, that had been leftover adrenaline from
the false alarm when the fireworks had exploded. For a second he'd been back in the heat of Bregnovia's civil war, his
life in danger along with the woman in his arms.

Shaking off that terrifying second of *not again,* he assured himself this urgency to see her again was merely his
libido looking for another easy pounce and feed.

That's why he'd had to force himself to take his time
rising and dressing in the cabana last night, despite a nagging desire to hurry. It wasn't that he'd wanted to catch
another glimpse, to actually catch *her* and convince her to
strip down completely and stay with him all night. No, he
was merely still horny.

Wondering why she hadn't stayed was pointless. He'd
never know. Everyone at *Q Virtus* had places to go and
people they preferred not to be seen with. Did she know
who *he* was, he wondered?

She hadn't been wearing a watch that he'd felt. He'd
checked his own as she'd left, trying to read her identifier
before she had moved out of range, but no luck. Perhaps
she'd run off to rejoin her husband or lover.

That thought infuriated him. Waiting to marry Luiza
until it was too late was one of his few regrets. When you
did make a lifelong commitment, you didn't break it. If
she had…

He refused to dwell on any of it. She was a wet dream
and he was awake now. Time to move on. He had an introduction to suffer through—would in fact drag his feet
getting there so as to use up most of their time.

Then he would put out feelers for the meeting he really
wanted. Someone here would know what was being said in
the UN about his country's chances for recognition. What-

ever he had to do to bestow legitimacy on his people, he would. They were his priority. It was Luiza's dream. He owed it to all of them to stay focused on that.

Not on some easy piece he'd picked up for a few hours of distraction.

Until the accident, Tiffany had always been fashionably—some would say chronically or even rudely—late. Once she began working, she'd discovered how irritating it was to be on the other side of that. Nowadays she strove to be early, and to that end she followed the directions on her watch, only to come up against yet another set of sliding doors. Rolling her eyes, she watched the timepiece count down how long she'd have to wait until they opened.

"Come on, come on," she muttered, wanting this meeting over with.

She'd almost forgotten it completely and wished she had. Unfortunately, her watch had been returned to her with her breakfast. "It was left in the reception lounge last night," Julio had said. "You have a message. That's what the blue light means."

"It was heavy and men kept coming up to me, saying my watch indicated I was open to being approached," she complained.

"Excellent feedback on the weight. A woman's perspective is so valuable for the manufacturers. But please let me show you how to set your Do Not Disturb."

He'd also shown her how to follow the directions to her meeting.

"Can I wear my mask?" she'd asked, peering at him from behind her feathers while trying to keep them out of her orange juice.

"Of course. Members typically wear their masks the entire time they're here."

With her main argument for blowing off the meeting disintegrated, she'd managed only a quiet, "Thanks."

Biting her thumbnail after Julio left, she'd debated whether to risk leaving her room. What if she saw *him?*

Heated tingles awakened, hinting at how exciting it could be to bump into him, but she tamped down on the wild feelings. Her behavior last night had been a crazy combination of being away from the stifling proximity of her family and, well, she had been a little drunk on rum, having almost finished her second drink by the time she'd begun dancing.

With a stranger.

Her lover.

A burble of near-hysterical laughter almost escaped her as she walked, thinking of their incredible encounter. Part of her reaction was delight that she had it in her to be that bold and daring. Before the accident she might have fantasized about something like that, but it would never be something she could imagine actually doing. There was no such thing as impulse in her family. The consequences to Daddy's career always had to be considered.

The rest of her giddiness had a sharply disappointed edge. This was the sort of secret she might share with a close girlfriend, but she didn't have any. Her friends, some closer than others, had all continued on with their lives during her recovery, living the life she was supposed to have. Hers had stalled and taken a sharp left turn. She would never have much in common with them now except the good old days. That topic just invited pitying stares.

Work was what she had now. A career. She had Paulie's corporation and men in her life who loved her as a daughter and a sister. Last night had been exciting and fun, but she couldn't repeat it. What was she going to do? Come to these events every quarter and sleep with a different stranger each time? The alternative, to expose her scars and hope a lover could overlook them, made her shudder in appalled dread.

No, she had to stay serious and focused and do what she'd been sent here to do. Last night was her personal secret, something to keep her glowing on the inside through the cold years to come. Today she represented Davis and Holbrook, one of the largest construction firms in the world, thanks to her marriage merging her father's architecture firm with Davis Engineering. As the one person with claim to both those names, she supposed she could take ten minutes out of her life to hand over the letter of introduction her brother had prepared.

Even if she didn't entirely approve of this man they wanted to court.

At least she could hide behind her mask. Kinky was her new normal, apparently, since she was becoming really fond of it, but it rejuvenated her confidence.

These gopher burrows under the building she was less sure of.

"Am I in an abattoir?" she asked a *petite q* when she found one.

"Absolutely not," the perky young woman replied, obviously not paid to have a sense of humor. "To ensure complete privacy for our guests, the doors only open if the next hallway is empty. Several people are moving around at this time, causing minor delays. Your meeting room is at the end of this hall and will open to your thumbprint."

As she stepped into the empty meeting room, however, she had to admit that this particular man's world was astounding. Given the industrial decor she'd traversed to get here, she had expected more of the same with the conference rooms. Instead she was in an aquarium—a humanarium—in the bottom of the sea. Stingrays flew like sparrows across the blue water over the glass ceiling and a garden of tropical fish bobbled like flower heads in a breeze, poking from the living reef that fringed the glass walls.

Amazed, she set down her black leather folder on a table between two chairs in the center of the room and walked the curved wall, keeping one hand on it to maintain her equilibrium as the distorted image of swaying kelp made her dizzy. She reminded herself to breathe and oriented herself by turning back to the room to take in the pair of chairs on the white area rug. They faced the windows and were separated by the table that held a crystal decanter of ice water and two cut-crystal glasses.

As she leaned her back against the window, the door panel whispered open and *he* stepped in. Her stranger.

Shock ran through her in an electric current that held her fixed, stunned.

Yes, that was the mask from last night, and she recognized his powerful build even though he was dressed differently. His gray shirt was short-sleeved, tailored close to his muscled shoulders and accentuated his firm, tanned biceps. The narrow collar of his shirt was turned down in a sharply contrasting russet, drawing her eye to the base of his throat.

She watched him swallow and lifted her gaze to his green-gold eyes.

How had he found her?

Behind him, the door whispered closed. The noise seemed to prompt him into motion. He took a few laconic steps into the room, hands going into his pockets. He wasn't taken aback by their incredible surroundings. His eyes never left their lock on hers as he paused next to the chairs, lifted a hand and removed his mask. He dropped it into one of the chairs, still staring at her.

Barefaced, he was beautiful. Not pretty, not vulnerable, but undeniably handsome with his narrow, hawkish face and sharply defined cheekbones. His blade of a nose accentuated the long planes of his cheeks to the rugged thrust of his jaw, making his mouth appear sensual by comparison, even though his lips weren't particularly full.

They weren't narrow, either, and neither were his eyes, but the keen way he watched her spoke of focus and intelligence.

Don't think about last night, she ordered herself, fighting the inner trembling of reaction.

"You could have given me your name last night and saved us taking up a room when they're so highly in demand."

Her throat closed as she processed his thick accent first. It was more pronounced when he spoke above a whisper and charged his deep, stern voice with husked layers. Then his words sifted through her mind, allowing her first to absorb that he recognized her, but didn't know her name. How—? The criticism in his tone penetrated, distracting her. She was rather sensitive to being called thoughtless, willing to admit she'd been quite the spoiled brat before she'd learned that even charmed lives could be hexed.

Finally she grasped the whole of what he'd said, and it sounded as if he thought she had known whom she was messing around with last night. Which meant he hadn't come here because he was looking for her, but because...

Oh. My. God.

"Ryzard Vrbancic?" she managed faintly. Please no.

His gorgeous mouth twisted with ironic dismay. "As you can see. Who are you?"

Of course she could see. Now that her brain was beginning to function, it was obvious this was the self-appointed president of Bregnovia. The leader of a resistance movement turned opportunist who had claimed the national treasury—from a fellow criminal, sure, but claimed it for himself all the same—then used it to buy his seat in his newly minted parliament.

How did a name such as Ryzard go from being something vaguely lethal and unsavory to noble and dynamic simply by encountering the man in person? How had she not sensed or realized—

"There's been a mistake. I've made a mistake." Oh, gawd, she could never tell her family. Her *virginity?* Really? To this man?

And yet her body responded to being in his presence. Even though she wasn't drunk and no music seduced her, her feet didn't want to move and her eyes kept being dragged back to his wide chest, where a sprinkle of hair had abraded her palms. His arms flexed as she watched, forcing memories of being caught protectively against him when the fireworks had started then carried like a wilting Southern belle when sex had been the only thing on their minds.

His wide-spaced feet in Italian leather drew her gaze, making her recall the way he'd shed his shoes and the rest of his clothes so deftly last night. His burnished bronze skin had been anything but cold and hard. He'd been taut and alive.

And generous. He'd touched her with incredible facility completely devoted to her pleasure. She tried not to look for his hands, but she was fervently aware of the way he'd tantalized her so intimately toward orgasm. In public.

Mortified heat burned her to the core, especially because she yearned to know it all again. Everything about him called to her, feathering over her nerves like last night's velvety breeze, not just awakening her sensuality, but exciting her senses into full alert. Why? How? The rapid plunge back into sexual arousal was incredibly confusing. Disconcerting. She needed to get out of here.

Pushing off the glass wall, she took two steps and he took one, blocking her.

Her heart plummeted through the floor. This undersea

garden had suddenly become a shark cage, and she was trapped inside it with the shark.

Warily she eyed him. "I didn't know who you were last night."

"No?" His brow kicked up, dismissing her claim as a lie.

"No!"

"You sleep with strangers often?"

"Apparently you do, so don't judge me."

His head went back a fraction, reassessing her. "Who are you?"

She folded her arms, debating. If she left now, without telling him, Christian might salvage something. She, of course, could never show her face in public again, but she didn't intend to. Except—

Her gaze involuntarily went to the black dossier on the table, the one that held their letter of introduction and a background on the company. She jerked her gaze back to his, panicked that he might have followed her look, but trying not to show it.

His vaguely bored gaze traveled to the table and came back to hers. Intrigue lit his irises, turning their green-gold depths to emerald. A cruel smile toyed with his mouth.

"That's not for you," she said firmly. "I have to go." She took one step toward the table and he reached without hurry to pick the dossier up.

"I said—"

He only flashed her a dangerous look that held her off and opened it with an elegant turn of his long finger. *Don't think about those fingers.*

Leave, she told herself, but there was no point. She couldn't outrun this sizzling mortification, no matter where she went. Her stomach turned over as she waited for a sign of his reaction to what he read.

A muted bell pinged. "Your reserved time has reached

its limit," a modulated female voice said through hidden speakers.

Thank God. Tiffany let out her breath.

"Extend it," Ryzard commanded.

"Will another thirty minutes be sufficient?"

"I can't stay," Tiffany insisted.

Grim male focus came up to hold her in place, locking her vocal chords.

"Send a full report to my tablet on Davis and Holbrook, specifically their director, *Mrs.* Paul Davis. Thirty minutes is plenty."

"Very good, sir." The bell pinged again and Tiffany thought, *run.* The threat he emanated seemed very real, even though he didn't move, only stared at her with utter contempt.

Bunching her fists at her sides, she lifted her chin, refusing to be anything less than indignant if he was going to jump to nasty conclusions about her. *He* could be married for all she knew—which was a disgusting thought. Her brain frantically tried to retrieve knowledge one way or another. She was no poli-sci major, but she'd always kept up on headlines, usually knowing way more than she wanted to about world politics because of her father's ambitions. There were gaps because of the accident, of course, months of news she'd missed completely that coincided with the coup in Bregnovia.

She had no memory about his marital status, but something told her he wouldn't be nearly so scornful of her if he had his own spouse in the wings.

Ryzard tossed the folder into the empty chair and hooked his hands in his pockets to keep from strangling the woman who wanted to play him for a fool. Her being married was bad enough. She might shrug off little things like extramarital affairs, but he did not.

The fact she thought she could buy his business was even more aggravating, partly because he was so affected by last night. As much as he wished he wasn't, his body was reacting to her even though she was dressed very conservatively. Her loose, sand-colored pants grazed the floor over heeled sandals he'd glimpsed when she had moved. They were clunky-looking things, but their height elongated her legs into lissome stems he wanted to feel through the thin fabric of her pants. Her yellow top was equally lightweight and cut across her collarbone, hiding skin that had seemed powder white last night.

What he'd seen of it, anyway. He couldn't see much today and found that equally frustrating. He might have detected her nipples poking against the fine silk of her top, but while her flat green jacket nipped in to emphasize her waist, it also shielded her breasts from his view.

Nothing about her appearance hinted at the exciting, sensual woman he'd met last night. Even her wild curls had been scraped back, which might have been an elegant display of her bone structure if he could see her face.

"Take off your mask," he ordered, irritated that his voice wasn't as clear as he'd like.

"No."

The quietly spoken word blasted into his eardrums. It was not something he heard often.

"It's not a request," he stated.

"It's not open for discussion," she responded, body language so hostile he could practically taste her antagonism.

Curious.

No. He wouldn't allow himself to be intrigued by her. Pulling himself together, he did his best to reject and eject her from every aspect of his life in one blow.

Glancing away as if his senses weren't concentrated upon her every breath and pulse, he said dismissively, "Tell your husband you failed. My business can't be bought. He might enjoy your second-rate efforts that offer no real pleasure, but I'm more discerning."

Her sharp inhale, as if she'd been stabbed in the lung, drew his gaze back to her. Her lips were white and trembled just enough to kick him in the conscience.

He forced himself to hold her hurt gaze, surprised how effective his insult had been. Her startling blue eyes deepened to pools of navy that churned with angry hatred. He didn't flinch from it, but instead held her gaze as if he was holding a knife in a wound, ensuring he would fully sever himself from a repeat performance of his weakness.

"How do you propose I tell him?" she asked with a bitterness that bludgeoned him, implacable and final. "Hire a psychic? He's dead." She pivoted to the door.

A blinding flash, like white light, shot through him. Not an external thing, but an inner slice of laser-sharp pain that he felt as an echo of hers. He knew that sort of grief—

Before he realized what he was doing, he'd moved to catch her arm and spin her around to him.

She used her momentum to bring her free hand up, sending it flying toward his face.

He caught her wrist and jerked back his head, his reflexes honed by war and a natural dominance that always kept him on guard. Still, a heavy blanket of regret suffocated him as he held her while she wordlessly struggled. He'd insulted her because he was angry, but he would never wound someone by dangling such a loss over them. An apology was needed, but holding on to her was like trying to wrestle a feral cat into a sack.

"Stop fighting me," he ground out, surprised by her wiry strength and unflagging determination.

"Go to hell!"

He got her wrists in one hand behind her back, her knee scissored between his own tightly enough to prevent it rising into his crotch. Squeezing her enough to threaten her breathing, he loosened off as she quieted.

"Big man, overwhelming a helpless woman," she taunted in a pant.

"You're not that helpless," he noted, admiring her fighting spirit despite his inherent knowledge that he shouldn't like anything about her.

She was widowed. That was tremendously important, even though he refused to examine too closely why he was so relieved. Or why he was now determined to learn more about her. He'd been serious about not being corruptible, no matter how his body longed to be persuaded.

Her shaken breaths caused her breasts to graze his chest, increasing the arousal their struggle had already stimulated. She recognized his hardness and squirmed again, forcing him to pin her even closer to hang on to her.

"Let me go," she said in a furious voice that provoked more than intimidated.

"In a minute." He reached to remove her mask—

She tried to bite him. He narrowly snatched his fingers from the snap of her teeth.

"You little wildcat." He couldn't help but be amused by her streak of ferocity. Her bared teeth were perfect, her pinched nostrils as refined as a spoiled princess's.

"I'm reporting this assault," she told him.

"I have a right to see whose body I was in last night," he told her, unconsciously revealing with the low timbre of his voice how disturbed he was by the memory.

"No, you don't. I'm discerning about who sees any part of me. And maybe I didn't bring my best game last night because I was bored and wanted it over with. Did you think of that?"

"I suppose I deserved that," he murmured, but her insult still landed like a knee in the gut, making his abdominal muscles clench in offense.

Digging his fingers around the knot of her hair, he tugged lightly, deliberately overwhelming her with his strength, exposing her throat and making her aware she was at his mercy. Not because he got off on hurting women. Never. But she needed to understand that even though she was utterly vulnerable to him, he wouldn't harm her.

"Now we've both said something cruel, and neither of us will do it again."

Her outraged "Ha" warmed his lips, making him deeply conscious of the shape of her Kewpie-doll mouth with its peaks in her top lip over a fat strawberry of a bottom one. Her scent, like Saponaria, somewhere between dewy grass and sun-warmed roses, threatened to erase all thought but making love to her again.

"I only said what I did because I thought you were married. And you tricked me. I don't like your trying to take advantage of me. To even the playing field…" He reached for the tailing ribbon that held her mask.

"Noooo." The sharp anguish in her voice startled him. She was genuinely terrified, straining into a twist to escape his loosening of the mask.

He let go of the ribbon and her, horrified that he'd scared her so deeply, but he couldn't help reaching to steady her when she staggered as she tried to catch the falling mask. Her shaking hands fumbled it before her, turning it around and around, trying to right it so she could put it on again. A desperate sob escaped her.

It was too late. He'd seen what she was trying to hide, and the bottom dropped out of his heart. He touched her chin, wanting a better look.

She knocked his hand away and flashed a look of fury at him. With her jaw set in livid mutiny, she stopped trying to replace her mask and stared him down with the kind of aggression that would make him fear for his life if she'd been armed.

"Happy?" she charged.

Not one little bit.

As he took in the mottled shades of pink and red, all he saw was pain. He'd been in battle. He knew what bullets and flames and chemicals could do to the human body. That's why his world had stopped last night when he'd thought a bomb was landing on the ramparts of the club.

But these were healed injuries, as well as they'd ever get anyway. The ragged edge of the facial scar followed a crooked line like a country's border on a map, sharply defining rescued flesh from the unharmed with a raised pink scar. It hedged a patch from over her left eye into the corner of her lid—she might have lost her sight, he acknowledged, cold dread touching his internal organs. Under her eye, it cut diagonally toward her nose before tracing down to the corner of her mouth and under her jawline, and then wound back to her hair.

The side of her neck was only a little discolored, but the way the color fanned at the base of it made him suspect the scarring went down her arm and torso, too, maybe farther.

As he brought his gaze back up to her face, he met eyes so bruised and wounded, he was struck with shame at causing her to reveal herself. He hadn't been trying to humiliate her. This wasn't meant as a punishment.

The hatred in her eyes took it as such anyway, stabbing him with compunction.

"I wouldn't work for you if your country was knocked back into the Stone Age and we were overinventoried in animal fur and flint. I'm leaving. Now."

He didn't try to stop her, sensing he'd misjudged her on a grand scale.

She tied her mask into place without looking at him. When she pressed the button to open the doors, they didn't cooperate, remaining closed while she swore at her watch.

"Tiffany," he cajoled, pulling her name from what he'd read, but not sure what he would say if he could persuade her to stay.

"Die," she ordered flatly.

The doors opened and she walked out.

CHAPTER FOUR

FOR THE FIRST time in months, Tiffany cried. Really cried as she hugged her knees in the shower and released sobs that echoed against the tiles. They racked her so hard she thought she'd throw up. She hated her life, hated herself, hated him.

She'd still been processing his remark about her efforts being second-rate when he'd yanked back her curtain and looked at her as if she was an object of horror. As though he was repulsed.

Sex was not worth this. Men weren't. She was old enough, and educated enough, to know that having a husband and kids were not necessary ingredients to a woman's happiness. Why then was she so gutted every time she was forced to face that no man would ever want her? That a family life would never be hers?

It was self-pitying tripe, and she had to get over it.

Forcing her weak legs to support her, she turned off the shower and leaned against the wall, cold and dripping until she worked up the energy to pull on a robe. As she moved into her room, she felt empty. Not better, not depressed, just numb.

That was okay. She could live with numb.

Perching on the foot of the bed, she stared at her wrinkled fingers and wondered what she should do. Hide in her room until this ridiculous clubhouse opened its doors

again? Fake appendicitis for a helicopter ride to the main-
land? She felt sick. She was damp and feverish, aching all
over, weak and filled with malaise.

A yawn took her by surprise and she thought, *Siesta.*
One small thing in her favor. Crawling up to her pillows,
she escaped into unconsciousness.

The sun crept around the edge of his balcony, likely to
begin blistering his bare toes soon, but Ryzard was ready
to stretch away the stiffness in his body anyway. He'd been
motionless for over an hour as he read through the report
he'd been provided by the *Q Virtus* staff.

Davis and Holbrook was an exceptional organization,
very well regarded in the international construction industry. He could definitely do worse as he looked at rebuilding
the broken roads and collapsed buildings in his city centers.
They had wanted to land on his radar as he moved toward
those sorts of goals, and now they were.

The rest of the report, about Mrs. Paul Davis, was even
more interesting. She had started out as a wealthy society
darling. Her marriage to a family friend had all the mark-
ings of a traditional fairy tale, right up to the wedding gown
with a train and the multitiered cake.

Except a wedding gift from the bride's brother of a
prestigious sports car had been more temptation than the
drunken groom could resist. He'd taken it up to ninety between the courtyard and the gates of the golf and country
club, detonating it against a low brick wall before the guests
had stopped waving.

After a flurry of death and memorial announcements
accompanied by touch-and-go mentions of the bride, the
reports had dried up. Fast-forward two years and his widow
was taking the reins of her dead husband's corporation. Her
brother had held her power of attorney during her recovery,
but his talents were better suited to hands-on architectural

engineering. The plethora of awards he'd earned spoke to that very loudly.

All of this would have been flat information if it didn't reinforce to Ryzard that he'd made a mistake in assuming she'd been trying to influence him with sex. What reason would she have? Her company was flourishing—somewhat surprisingly, given that her credentials amounted to an arts degree and attitude, but her grades were exceptional. She was certainly intelligent.

And he could personally attest that she was a ballbuster, he allowed with irony. He had no doubt she was more than a figurehead. If she had a vision, quite likely one formed in her husband's name, she would achieve it.

Turning from that disturbing thought, he allowed that if Bregnovia had already attained recognition, she might have tried for an advantage while he had a wider playing field to draw from, but it would be a risky move until his government was recognized.

Did their interest in his business mean an acknowledgment for Bregnovia was in the works? Or was their rendezvous exactly what it seemed to be: two healthy people enjoying the pleasures of the mating ritual.

Heat pooled in his lap as he dwelt on the possibility she'd welcomed him because she'd been as caught up as he had in their physical compatibility.

A twinge of conscience followed, but he had long ago rationalized that his heart and his body were separate when it came to sex. He had the same basic needs as any living thing, requiring nutrition, a sheltered environment and a regular release of his seed. If a peculiar mix of chemistry intensified his reaction when that last happened, well, he couldn't be held responsible. It was hormones, not emotion.

It was not infidelity against Luiza.

And Tiffany would have no reason to pursue him for sex

to gain his business. It would only complicate what might otherwise be a wise and lucrative association.

Something he should take under consideration, he supposed, scraping the side of his thumb against the stubble coming in on his jaw. It didn't matter how he cast their tryst. It shouldn't happen again.

Except there was one other fact from this report that kept teasing him.

Mr. Holbrook, Tiffany's father. An architect by education, he'd quickly become a career politician who'd worked his way up the ranks of local councils into a senator's mansion. He was now running for the presidency.

Suppose last night had been pure coincidence. Why then had the Holbrooks requested he meet them here, under the discreet curtain of *Q Virtus?* If they feared making a play for his business would hurt the senator's chances, they wouldn't have met him at all. No, it must mean they knew the United States was leaning toward recognition.

A flush of excitement threatened to overtake him, but Ryzard reminded himself to be patient. Backing from the United States would influence many other countries to vote in his favor, but nothing was confirmed.

Still, one thing was clear: he needed another meeting with Tiffany Davis.

Tiffany woke foggy-headed to a noise in the main room like dishes rattling on a cart. Leaping from the bed, she staggered to the door into the lounge and found Ryzard Vrbancic directing one of the *petite q's* to set a table on the balcony.

"What are you doing?" She turned the lapel of her robe up against her cheek.

"I thought you were showering, but apparently you went back to sleep."

"What?" Tiffany scowled at him. "How do you know

what I've been doing? I thought these rooms were completely secure," she charged the woman in the red gown.

"I used my override to bring in the meal you ordered… didn't you?" The young woman looked suspiciously at Ryzard, but he was quick.

"We did, thank you. I'll manage from here. You can go." To Tiffany, he said, "Don't confuse the staff just because we've had a tiff." A mild snort and, "You're aptly named, aren't you?"

"Get out of here," she cried.

The *petite q,* already hurrying, ran to the door and out.

Goggling at Ryzard, whose mouth twitched, Tiffany said, "Seriously?"

"You're overreacting."

"I want you to leave."

"I'm about to make you an offer you can't refuse. Quit hiding and accept."

She narrowed her eyes on his back as he moved onto the balcony, not interested in anything from him except assurances her family would never find out what had happened between them. Not that she was willing to say so.

It took everything in her to stand tall and say, "What kind of offer?" She was writhing inside at everything that had happened, yet had wound up dreaming about him. It had been erotic until it had turned humiliating.

"I can't hear you," he called from the balcony.

Clenching her teeth, she wavered in the doorway, hanging back while telling herself not to let him get away with this manipulation. At the very least, she ought to cover up. She didn't so much as go for milk in the middle of the night without concealer for fear of frightening the staff at home. The only reason she'd forgone it this morning was because she'd expected to keep her mask on.

Ryzard Vrbancic had seen her, however, and she was

still flopping like a fish out of water, gasping for air, waiting for the boot that would send her careening off the boat.

Everything in her cringed with a need to hide, but maybe seeing her again like this would repel him into moving along.

Yanking tight the tie on her robe, she marched to the open French doors and said, "I'm not interested in any offers from you. Please leave."

"I thought you were dressing," he remarked, squeezing fresh lemon across raw oysters in their half shell. They were arranged on a silver tray of ice. Next to them sat a tapas platter of fritters, flatbread, shredded meat, guacamole, salsa and something that looked like burritos but they were wrapped in a type of leaf.

Her stomach growled. She tried to cover the sound with her hand, but he'd heard.

"You're hungry. Eat," he urged magnanimously. As if he wasn't trespassing in her room.

"I prefer to eat alone." She indicated the door, not subtle at all.

He picked up an oyster and eyed her as he slurped it into his mouth, chewed briefly, then swallowed. Raw oysters were supposed to be an aphrodisiac. She'd always thought they were disgusting, but what he'd just done had been the sexiest thing she'd ever seen. She followed the lick of his tongue across his lips, and a wobbly sensation accosted her insides.

Reacting to him made staring him down even more difficult than it already was, but she held his gaze, inner confidence trembling as she waited for another flinch to overtake him like the one this morning. His expression never wavered, though. He let his gaze slide to her scarred cheek, but then it went south into her cleavage, where the swells of her breasts peeped from between her lapels. His perusal continued over her hips, lingered on the dangling ends of her belt and ended at her shins, one white, one mottled.

Involuntarily, her toes curled as she reacted to his masculine assessment. She couldn't tell if she was passing muster or being found wanting. She told herself it didn't matter, that she didn't want his approval or any man's, but in her heart she yearned for a hint of admiration.

He pulled out a chair. "Sit down."

Swallowing, telling herself to keep a straight head, she deliberately provoked a reaction to her flaws by saying, "I'm not supposed to go in the sun."

He shrugged off the protest. "It will set in twenty minutes."

"Look, I'm running out of ways to tell you to get lost without pulling out the big one. I don't want anything to do with you. I was against giving you that letter in the first place, and I'm sorry I came here at all. We won't work for you."

He finished another oyster, but she had his full attention. She could feel it. When his tongue cleaned his lips, she imagined he was licking her all over.

Ignore it, she chided herself.

"Why?" he asked.

Why what? Her brain had lost the plot, but she quickly picked it up, reminding herself of *his* flaws.

"Because I don't like your methods. You're no better than the criminal you replaced."

"I'm a lot better than the criminal I replaced. Check my human-rights record," he growled while a flush of insult rose to his cheeks.

It was enough antagonism to give her pause and make her reconsider deliberately riling him, but despite how much she hated herself for having sex with him, she was still aware of a pull. She desperately needed to cut him down and out.

"You're living pretty large while your countrymen starve. How many people died so you could eat raw oysters and watch the sun set?"

"You know nothing about what I've lost so my people can eat," he said in a lethal tone.

As he spoke, he turned aside to toss his empty shell on the cart, but she glimpsed such incredible pain she caught her breath against an answering stab of anguish. She quickly muffled it, but something in her wavered. Was she misjudging him?

She shook off the thought, scoffing, "Did I strike a nerve? Do you not like having your repulsive side exposed?"

He shot her a fierce look and she thought, *Shut up, Tiffany*.

"You're acting out of bitterness, and it's not with me. We promised not to be cruel."

That gave her a niggle of guilt, which she didn't like at all. She looked at her perfectly manicured nails.

"You might have promised," she said haughtily. "I didn't."

"You like to deliberately hurt people? You do have an ugly side."

That lifted her gaze, and his expression made her heart tremor where it clogged the base of her throat. He had very patrician features. Very proud and strong. Right now they were filled with contempt.

Shame lunged in her. She might have been spoiled and self-involved, but she never used to be mean. But she was angry. So angry. And there was no one to take it out on. She had to look away from the expression that demanded she apologize.

She wavered, uncertain of her footing, but she had enough unscrambled brain cells to remember he was a dictator, not some do-good pastor.

"What do you expect, a welcome mat?" she hazarded, tucking her fists behind her upper arms, affecting a bravado she didn't feel. "You've invaded my territory—"

"You're not angry I'm here. You're angry you had to face the man you made love to last night. That I saw your secret. You're not repulsive, Tiffany."

"As I said, you're stepping into places you haven't been invited."

"I was invited." He picked up an oyster, and his tongue curled to chase and catch the slippery flesh before he pulled the morsel into his mouth.

Inner muscles that were still vaguely tender from their lovemaking clenched involuntarily, sending a shimmer of pleasure upward to her navel and down the insides of her thighs.

When he took a step toward her, she took a hasty one back, bumping into the rail of the balcony.

He raised his brows as he pulled out her chair another inch, reading way too clearly what kind of nervousness she'd just revealed.

"I want you to leave," she insisted.

"We'll clear the air first."

She almost mumbled an adolescent, *I don't want to clear the air.* Because she didn't. She wanted to hit and bite and push away.

She wanted to be left alone to die of loneliness.

Oh, don't be such a baby, Tiffany.

It was true, though. She was like a wounded animal that snarled at anyone who tried to help it. It was the source of the horrible tension with her family. They didn't know what to do with this new Tiffany who hated her life and everything in it.

She glared at Ryzard, loathing him for being the man to show her how twisted she'd become. He'd caught her in a moment of terrible weakness last night, playing pretend that she was normal. He'd sliced past the emotional scar tissue she'd grown, and he seemed to still be doing it. That made him dangerous.

"The sun is about to set. It won't hurt you to be out here," he said.

She whipped around to see how close it was to the horizon. She hadn't been in the sun for more than a handful of steps between a house and car in two years. As she stepped into its rays, the heat on her face felt good. The fading red ball filled her with rapture as it lowered toward the sea.

Holding her breath, she strained her ears.

The band started below, making her slap a hand on the rail in disappointment. "I wanted to hear it!"

"Hear what?" he asked, standing next to her.

"When the sun touches the water."

He gave her a skeptical look that said, *Aren't you a bit old for that?*

She turned away, hiding that yes, she clung to certain childish fantasies that reminded her of easier, simpler times. Being lighthearted and silly didn't come naturally to her anymore, and she desperately longed to find that part of herself again. Tiny moments of happiness were like bread crumbs, hopefully leading her back to a place of acceptance. Maybe even contentment.

"You're really quite sensitive, aren't you?" he mused.

"No."

"And contrary." He waved at the chair he'd pulled out for her. "I have some questions for you. They're important. Sit."

"I'm not a dog."

"No, you're as aloof and touchy as a wet cat. The purring version is worth all the scratching and hissing, though."

"I don't want to talk about that," she rushed to state, unnerved by the suggestiveness in his remark.

"We won't. Not yet," he agreed, and his touch on her shoulder nudged her to sit.

She did, mainly to avoid the way the light contact of his hand made her stomach dip in excitement, and partly because her mother was lecturing her in her head. The members of their family, in all their greatness, were ambassadors, obligated to set an example of good manners and rising above the unpleasant. Such an annoying legacy.

She was also starving. Taking care of herself had become a habit through her recovery. Good food was one of her few real pleasures these days, and this stuff looked awesome.

He watched her build a flatbread into a soft taco, not being shy with the high-calorie avocado paste, either.

"What?" she asked defensively.

"I'm not used to seeing a woman eat like that."

She bit back a spiteful, *Too busy watching them starve?* She really didn't want to be that person, but she didn't know how else to handle him.

"Why are you here?" she asked instead.

He paused in preparing his own flatbread. "Why are *you* here, Tiffany? Why did your family send you to meet me?"

The weight of his gaze turned her shrug into a shiver. "Apparently I'm the only one who is a member."

His brows went up in surprise.

"I inherited my husband's fortune. My father isn't exactly struggling, but he doesn't qualify."

"I read about your accident. I'm sorry for your loss."

She prickled, waiting to see if he would make more of it, dig deeper, question how a married woman could have been a virgin.

"I'm also a member and was one long before our civil war. The money you accuse me of stealing is Bregnovia's. It's earmarked to fund our recovery."

She eyed him, seeing a contrary mix of Euro-sophistication and obdurate leader. When he caught her looking at him, her heart skipped. She looked away.

"I'll have to request a report on you from the powers that be. Find out how you made your fortune," she said.

"I'll tell you. It's a spigot system I developed for the oil industry, inspired by what I learned working in vineyards after finishing my engineering degree."

Despite her inner warnings to hold him off, she was intrigued. "That seems an odd choice. What was an engineer doing in a winery?"

"Rebelling," he said flatly, not inviting more questions as he reached to the wine bucket and drew out a dripping green bottle. "This is from my country. You'll enjoy it."

Of course she would. Who would dare not?

His arrogance was growing on her if she was finding it more amusing than annoying.

"What do you mean, you were rebelling?"

He drew a subtle breath, as though gathering himself for something difficult. "If you were to order a report on me, you would learn my parents sent me to live in Germany when I was six. For my safety and to give me a better life. Our country has been annexed by one neighbor or another since before the First World War. There were constant outbreaks of independence-seeking followed by terrible repression. My parents couldn't leave, but they smuggled me out to friends. I can't complain. My foster parents were good people. The husband was an automotive engineer who pressed me to follow in his footsteps. As a vocation I didn't mind it, but when I graduated I felt as most young people do. That this was my life and I could do as I liked." He shrugged, mouth twisting in self-deprecation. "I'm not proud of abandoning my potential to pick grapes, but it allowed me to bring a fresh perspective when I went to Russia, planning to make my fortune drilling for oil."

"Where you fashioned this doodad that is so popular it made you into a bazillionaire?"

"Da," he confirmed with a nod.

"Humph." She reached for her wine. "Does the rest of the world know this?"

He lifted a shoulder dismissively. "The press prefers to sensationalize what I did with my money."

"Which was to fund a war."

"I freed my country."

"And now you own it."

"I lead it. What do you think of the wine?"

She was no sommelier and didn't bother with sniffing and swirling, but she thought the light color was appealing and she enjoyed the way the initial tang, almost fruity, eased into something more earthy. Not oaky. Vanilla?

She tried again, wanting to determine what it was. But as much as she loved wine, alcohol had been off-limits as her body had needed every advantage to recover. That made her a lightweight. She had to be careful about losing her head around him.

As the memory of their dirty dancing and everything that followed bathed her in heat, the proximity of a bedroom and sitting here in her robe suddenly seemed incredibly dangerous and intimate.

Ryzard watched a glow of awareness brighten Tiffany's skin, filling her compelling blue eyes even as she looked into the crisp white wine she set aside. Her reaction might be in response to the alcohol, but his male instincts read her differently.

He shifted in his chair, widening his knees to make room for the growing reaction tugging insistently between his legs.

Tricking the waitstaff into granting him entry to her room had been the oldest one in the book, but as he'd suspected, she wouldn't have seen him otherwise and he wanted answers. At this precise second, however, he found himself with only one thing on his mind: her. She was more complex than he'd given her credit for, both when he'd lost himself in the mecca of her flesh and when he'd assumed she was attempting to manipulate him.

She was far more beautiful than he'd taken the time to notice this morning, too. Then his attention had been drawn to the scarring, his focus on the pain it indicated. Now he could see what had existed before discoloration and a raised jagged line had bisected her cheek. Blonde, blue eyed, with skin like a baby and the bone structure of an aristocrat, she was Helen of Troy.

Not that he was prepared to go to war ever again, but he could imagine men who would. Her young husband must have been intimidated, knowing how coveted she was.

"It's rude to stare," she said, growing redder in one cheek.

"I'm not staring. I'm admiring."

Her mouth shrank in rejection, and so did his brain. He forced himself to look away from thick lashes that swept down to hide her eyes. This meeting wasn't about kindling an affair that had barely started, no matter how much the thought appealed.

It appealed far too much. He could barely concentrate as memories of her pushing her ass into his groin as she writhed with pleasure under his slippery touch filled his head. The heady power of fondling her to orgasm had made him drunk and was overshadowed only by how good she had felt squeezing him in her hot, perfect depths.

But his country came first. He couldn't forget that. Couldn't forget anything.

He shook himself out of his fascination and spoke briskly.

"Your father seems exceptionally well connected in Washington. By sending you to speak to me, he is signaling that your country is likely to support my petition for recognition at the UN, is he not? Has he told you this is forthcoming?"

"He's under that impression, but who knows what the attitude will be tomorrow? Welcome to politics. You know how these things work."

He did, and the hardest lesson he had learned after being in a war was when to back off and use diplomacy instead of force to get what he wanted. It was also standard practice to weigh a person's impact on an agenda before developing a relationship.

Maybe he hadn't properly examined how their affair could affect his goal before he made love to her, but Tiffany's knowledge and connections suggested she could have a very positive influence.

A wild rush of excitement flew through him as he found a rationale to continue their affair, but he forced himself to hold on to a cool head and gather information first. "Does your father have any sway over your country's decision makers?"

"He has followers. Believers in his vision. Isn't that how you got elected, by cultivating the same?" The remark was somewhere between haughty and ironic.

"You don't seem to be one of them. His followers, I mean. It's quite obvious you're not one of mine. Yet."

"Ha," she choked, but she lowered her lashes as if to prevent him reading something different in her eyes. "Never yours and while I'll always cheer for Dad, I'm tired of living my life by his career," she said with dour humor and popped a cherry tomato into her mouth, pursing her lips in a pout as she chewed.

"When is the election?" he asked, trying not to watch her plump lips too closely.

"Not for a year, but the campaigning is well under way. He was leaving for Washington as we were coming here."

"We?" he asked sharply, territorial instincts riled.

"My brother and I."

"Ah. That's fine then." He frowned. Whatever relief he felt in knowing there wasn't another man in her life was buried under the discomfort of revealing he saw himself in the role. What was it about her that not only affected him but also lowered his ability to hide how much?

She lifted her brows. "Jealous?" Her smile was taunting, but her voice thinned across the word, suggesting a vulnerability that further undermined his resistance to her.

He shouldn't want her this badly, but he did. Last night had been exceptional, and she was a practical connection to cultivate. Where was the sense in fighting it?

"Possessive," he corrected. "You have a lover, *draga.*"

Her shocked expression masked into something complex. Her lips tightened in dismay while her brow flinched in pain. A stark yearning drew her features taut while her swallow indicated a type of fear. Then it all smoothed away, leaving him unsettled, wondering if an affair with her could become more complicated than it needed to be.

"Had," she said in a husky voice. "Past tense."

"I'm not talking about your husband," he growled, stirred to jealousy after all.

The blank look she sent him disappeared in a raspy laugh. "Neither am I."

His sharp brain caught a hidden meaning, but she kept talking, distracting him.

"Last night was a departure from my real life, not something I'll ever do again. Why would you even want to—" Dawning comprehension waxed her features before her face gradually tightened in rejection and something more disturbing. Anguish. "Wow. Nice to know some things haven't changed," she said bitterly.

"What do you mean?" Clammy palms seemed an overreaction to being rejected as a one-nighter. He'd done it himself in the past, but he didn't like it. Not from her.

"I'm still capable of being used," she answered. "You think that if you keep me close, you'll keep my father's cronies closer."

A pinch of compunction gave him pause, but that's not all that was going on here. And now she'd piqued his curiosity.

"Who used you in the past? How?" It was a tender point for him. Only a blind fool would fail to see the advantage to him in associating with her, but there were lines, especially with women. When Luiza was taken, it was to use her as leverage against him. She'd ended her life to prevent it. He never took manipulation of the unwilling lightly.

"Who *hasn't* used me?" she demanded. "I thought if there was one silver lining to this—" she drew a circle around her face "—it was that I was no longer a pawn. Thanks for dinner." She stood up, tossing him a pithy look. "A girl in my position is lucky when a man shows her a bit of attention. You're a helluva guy, Ryzard."

Her contempt burned like acid as it dripped over him. It might not have seared so deeply if he hadn't grasped at the advantages of an affair to justify exactly how badly he wanted to continue theirs.

He didn't want to admit how fierce his hunger for her was, but the hurt beneath her words told him she didn't see any at all. Wounding her, especially when she was so sensitive about her desirability, had a disturbing effect on him. Guilt assailed him and provoked something deeper. A compulsion to draw her close and make up with her.

He didn't want to be so enthralled. It went against everything he'd promised himself and Luiza's memory. Nevertheless, he reacted to the way she rejected him with a pivot of her body. It incited him to strike fast to keep from being shut out. Fear that had nothing to do with the best interests of his country goaded him to act.

"Don't underestimate what's between us, Tiffany." He

inwardly cringed at revealing so much, but he was even more averse to her thinking he was capable of low motives. "The attraction between us is real and very strong."

"Oh, give it up! You don't want me. You—"

"Shall I prove it?" He rose and easily stalked her across the tiny space of the balcony, using her outstretched hand to tug her close and pulling her resistant body into to his own.

"What do you think you're doing?" she demanded, wriggling for freedom then stilling when she felt his arousal. "You—" Confusion stilled her and she searched his expression.

"As I said." He lowered his head, setting a determined kiss over her protesting mouth.

Tiffany continued to press for distance, but he wasn't being mean, just insistent. Still, she was awfully confused. The way he'd given her that moment of hope that she could be attractive to someone before she realized it was all a ruse had been devastating. Now he was coming on strong, making her want to melt into him. Really, seriously, turn to mush in his arms. It was so frightening to be this affected. She did the only thing she could think to do. She tried to bite him.

He jerked his head back. "Are we playing rough, *draga?*" He shot his hand beneath her robe, grasping her breast in a firm hand, dislodging the slippery tie of her robe so it started to fall open.

"Don't!" she cried, hunching and scrambling to keep as much cloth in place as possible. "Please, Ryzard, don't do this. Not out here where anyone could see."

He froze, then slowly withdrew his hand. The tips of his fingers grazed a distended nipple, sending a pulse of pleasure-pain through her. She was too humiliated to respond and too shaken by the fear of exposure to appreciate his obeying her plea.

"Tiffany," he scolded as he held her in loose arms. "I'm not trying to hurt you."

Pushing back until he reluctantly let his hold on her drop away, she ensured she was completely covered, but couldn't lift her head.

"I've seen battle scars, you know." The hand he used to smooth her hair back from her bad cheek was surprisingly compassionate.

Rather than turn into his caress, she averted from it.

"I'm your first lover since the accident? That's why you're so shy?" Ryzard was still trying to catch up to the way her shield of toughness had fallen away so quickly into such tremendous vulnerability. One second she'd been a worthy adversary, the next a broken fawn in need of swift protection.

"Yeah." Her snorted word held a hysterical note. She tried to step over the chair he'd upended, trying to move away from him. Tears sheened her eyes, her emotions so close to the surface he knew she was near a tipping point.

He bent to right the chair, allowing her to move away into privacy because pieces were falling into place in his mind in a way he couldn't quite believe. Her back seemed incredibly narrow and bowed under a weight as she entered the suite. He could hardly countenance what he was think-ing, but her gasp of pain last night rang in his ears. He had thought she just wasn't quite ready, but...

Cautiously he followed, one hand going to the door frame to steady himself as he asked, "Tiffany. Am I your *only* lover?"

She didn't turn around, but her shoulders seemed to flinch before she lifted her head to say cockily, "So far, but with my looks and connections, I'm encouraged to believe there's more in my future."

He bit back a curse while his free hand clenched into a

fist at his side. He wanted to shake her out of sheer frustration with her cavalier attitude, but at the same time he had a deep compulsion to cradle her against him. The erotic memory of their coming together grew sweeter even as he struggled with the ramifications of being a woman's first. He'd done it once before. He knew the emotional ties it pulled from both parties.

A splintering sensation accosted him as he once again compared her with Luiza. His first instinct was to walk away. Confusing emotions tumbled through him like a rockslide, tainted with the intense grief he'd managed to avoid as the aftermath of war had consumed him. He once again hated himself as a traitor for having more than a passing interest in Tiffany, but learning he was her first changed things. He wasn't so archaic he thought virginity was a seal of quality, but losing it was an important marker in a woman's life. He couldn't be dismissive of her or what she'd offered him, even if she was trying to be.

"Can you explain to me how this is possible, *Mrs*. Davis?"

Tiffany looked to the ceiling, battling back stupid tears and a deeper sense of vulnerability than she'd ever felt. There had been a time when her confidence, her belief in her own superiority, had been unflagging. In an instant she had become weak and broken and dependent. Finding her way back from that seemed impossible, and she hated that Ryzard saw her at this low point. He was so strong and sure of himself. Where had he been when she'd had all her defenses in place and could have handled his forceful, dynamic personality?

A dozen sarcastic responses to his question came to her tongue, but the nearest she could get to flippant was to say, "I was afraid I'd fall in love with someone else if I didn't save myself for Paulie."

She tightened her belt and turned, surprised to catch him in an unguarded moment.

The faraway look in his eye suggested he had dark thoughts of his own. Seeing he might not be as completely put together as he seemed gave her the courage to continue with more outspokenness than she'd ever allowed herself.

"Our marriage was written in stone. Our fathers were friends, and his mother was my mom's maid of honor. Paulie and my brother, Christian, were inseparable through childhood. The architect and engineer designed the bridge between our families when Paulie and I were still in diapers. By the time I was in high school, no other boy had the guts to ask me out. They knew I was already taken."

"You didn't date? Didn't sleep with him?"

"*Paulie* dated. He sowed enough wild oats for the both of us. He took me to the Friday night dances, and on Monday I would hear what had happened at the parties he went to after he dropped me at home. He came *here* and had affairs."

"And you put up with that?"

She sighed, hugging herself. "I believed him when he told me he was getting it out of his system. He swore that once we were married, he would never stray. I still believe he meant it. He encouraged me to do the same," she offered with a shrug, "but like I say, no one offered and I told myself it would be romantic to wait."

"Did you love him?"

She sighed, chest aching as she admitted what she'd never told anyone. "I adored him like a best friend. That's a good foundation for a marriage, right?" She had needed to believe it, but hearing it now only made her hug herself tighter.

She tried to stem the emotions swelling in her, but the rest of her feelings, the churning doubts and anger and grief, gathered and poured out. "I miss him like crazy. He's the one person who would have been right beside me through all of this, keeping my spirits up, saying all the right things. But I don't know if I'd even be speaking to him because I'm so angry. I hate him for dying, really truly hate hi—"

A sob arrived like a commuter train with a whoosh and a suck of air. She held herself steady as grief rose and peaked. She blinked and trembled until she could assimilate it. After a long minute, she found control again and managed to continue.

"I hate him for getting behind the wheel that night. I hate Christian for giving him the car. I hate myself for thinking one spin up the drive when we were all so drunk would be okay."

Something tickled her jaw, and she realized a tear had bled down her numb cheek to burn her chin. She swiped it away and sniffed back the rest.

Through blurred eyes, she saw Ryzard looked gray, but she was coming back from a dark place. The whole world looked dull and bleak.

"I've never admitted that to anyone," she confessed. "I think it needed to come out. Thank you." She rubbed her arms, becoming aware she was frozen and achy.

Ryzard's long legs and wide chest appeared unexpectedly before her. He drew her into his arms even as she drew a surprised breath. His expression was stark and filled with deep anguish.

"Don't say anything," he said heavily, overcoming her automatic stiffening and pressing her into the solid strength of his body. "Just be quiet a minute."

He smoothed hands along her back to mold her into him, warming her. It wasn't a pass. It was comfort. After a hesitant moment, she let her head settle into the hollow of his shoulder and closed her eyes. He stroked her hair and she let her arms wrap around him, hugging him so the bruise that was her heart still ached, but felt covered and protected by the shield of his solid presence.

"Sometimes anger and hatred are the only things that get you through the injustice," he said so quietly she wasn't sure she really heard him, but the tickle across her hair told her his voice was real. "I envy people of strong faith. They never seem tortured by the why of it."

She swallowed, floored to realize they were sharing a moment, something so deep and personal it didn't need a name of a lost one for her to know he understood her utterly and completely. He suffered as she did.

Her hand moved on his back, soothing the tension in the muscles alongside his spine. She relaxed into him and they held each other for a long minute.

Gradually she realized he was becoming aroused. He wasn't overt about it, but she knew and an answering thread of response began subtly changing her own body. Her internal organs felt quivery and her breasts grew sensitive. Awareness of their stark physical differences expanded in her mind along with how intimately they'd fit themselves together last night.

As heat suffused in her, she tried to pull away and keep her head ducked so he wouldn't see how she was reacting.

He kept her close and tilted her face up. His mouth twitched ruefully, but his eyes remained somber. "You see?" he murmured. A sensation of pressure made her think he might have stroked his thumb over the scar tissue on her cheek. "We're a good fit. You should let me give you the after-party you deserved before your wedding."

"Tempting," she said, backing out of his hold because a resurgence of warmth that had its feet in embarrassed longing tingled through her. "But I'm not a charity case you need to offer a pity lay. Give me your email and I'll let you know if my father learns anything."

"My desire for you has nothing to do with my political

agenda," he dismissed with a heavy dollop of annoyance. "I want you."

She snorted. "Why?"

"Because, Tiffany, if you had any experience with men, you would know that last night was remarkable. There are people who have been together years and not been so attuned to each other." He flinched a little as he said that, but she was too busy reacting to his outrageous claim.

"That's not what you said this morning." She tried to sound unaffected, but she was still feeling unfairly spanked. It reflected in the raspy edge on her tone and filled her with debasement long after the insult had landed. She couldn't even look at him.

"I was under a wrong impression and behaved unpleasantly. I apologize."

She eyed him, skeptical.

"I don't apologize often. I suggest you accept it."

"No doubt," she allowed with a twitch of her lips. His arrogance ought to turn her off, but he seemed to have a right to it. His inner strength was as compelling as his obvious physical virility. When it wasn't turned against her, that combination was lethally attractive.

"Come here," he cajoled in a smoky invitation, even though he stood within touching distance and only had to reach out if he really wanted to.

"Why?" She stayed where she was, but everything in her gravitated to him.

"I want to kiss you. Show you how good we are together."

"Seduce me?"

He offered a masculine smile so tomcattish and predatory, it made her stomach dip in giddy excitement. "I would very much like to make love to you again," he said.

An image of her naked body, the one she avoided in the

mirror every day, flashed in her mind. She drew the lapels of her robe together and shook her head.

"Find someone else. I'm not playing hard to get. I just don't see the point."

Rather than argue, he pursed his mouth in regret. "I've damaged your trust in me."

"There wasn't much to begin with," she assured him with a tight smile.

"And the claws are revealed once again." He seemed more amused than irritated. "You trusted me enough to share your—what does your American singer call it? The wonderland that is your body."

"Yes, well, I was pretending to be someone else," she dismissed with false breeziness, inner foundations unsteady as she recalled how completely she'd deluded herself into believing what she'd done was okay.

"Do it again," he commanded.

"Ha!" She couldn't help it. The man was so lofty and single-minded.

"I'm serious," he insisted. "Put on your mask. We'll go downstairs and find that woman capable of such delightful spontaneity."

"It's—no. I can't."

But she couldn't think why. At least, not fast enough to have an answer ready when he demanded, "Why not?"

"Because…" She searched for a reason.

"We could dance again. We both enjoyed that. Of course, we could do that here." He glanced to where the balcony doors stood open. The music from the band below drifted in with the sea-scented air and the swish of waves on the shore.

The mood and music came across as a lazy, exotic throb.

"No," she said firmly, smart enough to be wary of his power once he got his hands on her. The way he'd felt her up on the dance floor last night had obviously been a spell of some kind.

"Downstairs it is. Shall we say one hour? I can shave and change in fifteen minutes, but you women need twenty just to find a pair of shoes."

"He said," she mocked, "demonstrating his vast experience with the opposite sex."

"I won't apologize. We're adults. We can enjoy each other if we want to." He moved forward to set a brief but profound kiss on her startled mouth. "Sure you don't want to stay in?" he asked in a private tone that made her blood flutter in her arteries.

Oh, she was tempted, but she shook her head. "I'm not sure I even want to see you again."

"Meet me downstairs, Tiffany, or I'll come looking for you. But I don't want to waste time searching. Set your watch."

She shook her head. "I don't like people thinking they can talk to me. I'd rather leave it on Do Not Disturb."

"Set it so *I* can find you." At her blank look, he gave her a head shake of exasperation. "Where is it? I'll show you."

A few minutes later she stood in her empty suite wondering how she'd gone from crying in the shower to having a date, one that made her feel more awake and alive than—this was dangerous—any other time in her life.

Oh, Tiffany, be careful. You could still fall for the wrong man.

No, she wasn't that pathetic and vulnerable, she assured herself. Nor was she strong enough to stay in her room and risk his coming for her. Besides, she had enjoyed feeling normal. There was no crime in that, was there?

She liked even more the idea of making him see her as beautiful. Turning, she went to see what treasures the designers might have left her.

CHAPTER FIVE

RYZARD MOVED THROUGH the three-dimensional images of a *carnivale* parade. He had to be careful. There were real people, *Q Virtus* members and *petite q's,* dressed as colorfully as the fake partiers, but for the most part he walked right through projections of extravagant floats and scantily clad women wearing beaded bikinis and feather headdresses. He stopped for a troupe of men in checkered pants and neon elephant masks when they began a tumbling routine in front of him, nearly convinced they were real.

His watch hummed, indicating Tiffany was close by, but *where?*

His need to see her again, to know she'd come down here for him, was out of proportion to any normal sort of anticipation. He brushed it aside, thinking if he could have her just once more, he'd be able to forget about her. It didn't matter that she'd revealed more about herself than he'd ever heard from all other *Q Virtus* members combined. Like most of the happenings here, their private conversation would stay locked in his own personal vault, not even to be revisited by him.

He especially refused to dwell on their comforting embrace when her mixture of grief and anger and self-blame had struck a chord in him. Even though, for the better part of a minute while he held her, he'd been at peace for the first time in a long time.

He stepped on a man's hands and looked through the feet that would have struck him in the nose if the vision was real. Music blared, voices cheered, and the holographic players were so dense he might as well have been in a crowd on the street.

There. All the hairs stood up on his body as he took her in.

She had her head bent to study her watch and pivoted as though trying to orient herself with a compass. The movement allowed him to take her in from all sides.

She really was strikingly beautiful. Tall and slender, but generously curved in the right places. He swallowed. She wore some kind of jumpsuit that clung from knees to elbows, then flared into ruffles down her forearms and over her shins. It had a subtle sparkle in its midnight blue color and clung to her ass so lovingly, his knees weakened.

He mentally recited the populations of Bregnovia's cities, trying to keep hold of his control as he approached her. Sidling up behind her, almost touching, he inhaled where she'd left the right side of her neck bare, gathering her hair to the left so it covered the scars.

"What the hell are you wearing?"

Her head came up. "You don't like it?" She jiggled the watch in her hand. "This thing was buzzing at me, but I couldn't figure out if you were over there or over there."

"I'm here," he growled, wanting so badly to palm the firm globe near his crotch his hand burned.

"So you are." She turned to study his mask from behind her own. "Hello again, Mystery Man. Buy me a drink? I've had a terrible day with the most arrogant, self-aggrandizing jerk you can imagine."

Few people could get away with insulting him so openly, but he found her brashness refreshing. Maybe even reassuring. She wasn't as vulnerable as she'd seemed in her suite. Good.

Testing the waters, he said, "I'm looking forward to one myself. I was stuck all evening with the most infuriating female, smart as a whip, but *blonde*. No offense." He tugged one of her ringlets.

For a moment her mouth stayed flat and humorless, just long enough for doubt to creep over his conscience. Then her lips twitched and a pretty, feminine chuckle erupted, sounding a shade rusty, as if she hadn't laughed unreservedly in a long time, but it engaged him in a way he hadn't expected. He instantly wanted to hear it again.

"None taken," she assured him breezily, turning to grasp his arm above his elbow, demonstrating how much self-assurance she possessed when she wasn't paralyzed by self-consciousness. "Can you believe this parade? I thought it was real."

Despite wanting to remark on the sudden change in her, he decided to go with it.

"The first time I saw this technology, it was a rain forest. It wasn't as robust as this, but the rain effect was quite something."

"You've been coming to these shindigs for a while?"

"This is my twenty-fifth. I earned a pin." He lifted his lapel to draw her eye to the small gold button.

"Nice. What does it do? Beam you up? Shoot lasers?"

"It tells people I belong."

Ryzard's mouth tightened after he spoke, as if he hadn't meant to reveal that, which piqued her curiosity all the more. "What do you mean?"

He shook his head, trying to dismiss her curiosity. "They have a live performance on the beach tonight. Shall we check it out?"

"Are you sensitive to not belonging because of the UN thing? You must know how slowly the wheels of political progress can turn. If the old boys' network is refusing to pick you for their team, tell them to stuff it."

His mask annoyed her. He was already pretty stoic, and now she had to try reading his emotions from the way the corner of his supersexy mouth flattened with disgust.

"I've learned to do exactly that, Tiffany. And it really doesn't matter to me if I'm rejected or found wanting, but I can't bear for my country to be discriminated against."

Discriminated. There was a big word. As a woman she'd been on the short end of that nastiness even in her own home in favor of her brother, but she couldn't imagine it happening to a man who showed so few weaknesses. He wasn't a typical representative of the people she understood to suffer the worst end of biases.

"When were you picked on? Why?" she asked, allowing him to steer her through the shower of candies that should have landed with a sting or crunched under her platform shoes.

He shrugged as if the details were inconsequential. "Different times. When I was a child and didn't yet speak German. I was late to sprout and quick to fight, angry that I couldn't see my parents. My temper was a problem. Getting a legitimate passport was a nightmare, so I was forever in a country illegally. That's one of the reasons I picked grapes. Things like visas can be overlooked when the fruit is ripe and a transient offers to help. But when I tried to go to America, they wanted nothing to do with me."

"So you went to Russia."

"There are parts as wild as your early frontier. Misfits are the rule."

"Which country's passport do you travel on now?"

"Bregnovian," he asserted, as if that should be obvious.

"But it's not recognized? That still keeps you from entering America?"

"I wouldn't be allowed into Venezuela."

"But you're welcome here." She pointed at the floor of the club.

He nodded once, still seeming bristly.

She considered how that might feel, always being separated and left out. Being who she was had always ensured her entrée into virtually any situation. For all her father's faults and detractors, he was still welcome everywhere. Even with her scars, she wasn't locked out. It was her choice to stay home.

She looked up at Ryzard, wanting to ask how he'd come to finally go home and fund a war, but they had arrived on the beach. Bending, she removed her shoes and allowed him to take them so she could walk barefoot in the cool, powdery sand.

"That's an excellent cover band," she said as they moved toward the music.

"It's the real band," he told her, making her chuckle.

He looked at her and the corners of his mouth curled again, but his mask and the strobing lights made it hard to tell if he was smiling because he was in a good mood, or if he was laughing at her.

"I can't get used to this," she excused. "It's a lot to pay just for an exclusive concert, isn't it? The membership fee, I mean."

"If you hadn't been sulking in your room, you could have attended some of the lectures. There was an excellent one on the situation in Africa. Last quarter, I brokered a free trade agreement that will ease a lot of strain on our wheat and dairy production."

She weighed that, seeing new value in these meetings and wondering if she would come to another. Maybe see him again.

Or see him with someone else.

The chasm that thought opened in her chest was so great,

she quickly distracted herself by declaring with false cross-ness, "I wasn't sulking."

"You're still pouting," he claimed and took her jaw in a firm hand, nipping her bottom lip with the firm but tender bite of his.

A zing of excitement shot straight down her breastbone into her abdomen, then washed tingles into her limbs. Her hands instinctively lifted to his waist, but she held him off by proclaiming, "I've heard that all my life. I can't help it if my bottom lip is fat."

He drew back enough to sweep a gaze of masculine appraisal across her masked features, then bent to take a slower, more detailed tour of her mouth, allowing them both the luxury of a small feast. Absently she shuffled toward him, knees and thighs shifting so he could fit their frames together. His erection pressed into her stomach and her breasts ached as she flattened them to his chest. The music seeped through her and he began to rock them in a slow dance.

More like making love to her in public again, but who cared? No one even knew who they were. God, he felt good under her roaming hands.

"Come to my room," he intoned against her good ear.

She had her hands fisted in his shirt beneath the jacket of his tuxedo. Everything in her wanted to hang on to him forever. It was such a dangerous precipice to stand on, so threatening of a bad fall. But she couldn't escape how good it felt to feel wanted and beautiful and capable of giving him pleasure.

Without even doing much soul-searching—just like last night—she offered a shaky nod and let him guide her back into the club then into an elevator where they kissed with barely schooled passion. A minute later, he thumbed the sensor that opened his door and pivoted her into the foyer of his suite. It was grander than her own, but he *was* a twenty-five-visit member. Still, she barely saw it. One second later, she was in his arms.

Knocking off his mask, he dipped his head and kissed her again, discipline abandoned as he let her know with the thrust of his tongue exactly what he wanted to do to her. His hands roamed over her restlessly and he finally jerked back to say, "What the hell is this thing? I can't find a zipper."

Which was why she'd chosen it, she recalled dimly. Even the neckline was a difficult entry point. She didn't have the courage to be naked with him, but she wanted to make love to him.

Smiling secretively, she fingered open the buttons of his shirt and gazed appreciatively at the sleek bronze chest plate she revealed. A narrow line of hair delineated the center of his chest and outlined his squared pecs, which were flat, firm statements of strength.

Above his left nipple, a scrolled phrase in blue ink gave her pause. Some of the letters were oddly accented, but she thought she read the word *Bregnovia*. Framing it with the finger and thumb of her splayed hand, she asked, "What does it say?"

Tension stole through him. He seemed to expend a lot of effort drawing in a pained breath. "Luiza, Martyr of Bregnovia."

"Like our Lady Liberty?"

She drew a circle around his nipple and he jerked, making her smile.

"Yes," he rasped. "She's revered—damn. By all."

Other questions crowded into her mind, but she was too distracted by his gorgeous physique. Her hands couldn't resist smoothing over the hot satin of his skin. "You're so perfect, Ryzard. It's intimidating."

"Take off your clothes," he urged, plumping her breasts through her spandex suit.

Cruising her hand from his waist to his belt and lower,

she explored the shape of him. He grunted with pleasure and was so hard against her palm, her internal muscles clenched in anticipation. She swallowed and used her other hand to fumble his pants open.

He tried to remove her mask, but she pulled away and shook her head. "Not yet." She was too intent on being the anonymous Tiffany, the one who followed impulse and seduced a man if she wanted to. Lowering his fly, she managed to expose him, and *oh*. She went to her knees because he made her so deliciously weak.

"Tiffany," he groaned raggedly.

She was barely touching him, too new at this to do more than brush light fingertips over him. His breaths were audible hisses of anticipation, his erection jumping in reaction to her caresses. When she smoothed her lips against silky skin over steel, the weight of his hand came to rest on her head. The other stroked her exposed cheek, fingers trembling.

An experimental lick imprinted her with the taste of him. This was new territory for her, something she'd always been curious about, but it was so much more enthralling than she'd expected. She could sense how much power she had as she learned his shape with her tongue and open-mouthed kisses

When she took the tip into her wet mouth, he growled a string of foreign words, guttural and tortured, but sexy and thick with pleasure. If she could have smiled, she would have. Instead, she focused on finding his sensitive points, wanting this to be something he would never forget.

She never would.

Ryzard managed to hitch his pants back into place, but wasn't capable of much else. His head was swimming, his muscles trembling, and he was too wrung out to properly close his fly. He needed the wall to keep himself upright.

Water ran in the powder room, but he was barely aware of anything else. What Tiffany had just done to him had blown his mind. Her inexperience had been obvious in her tentative touch and first nervous licks, but after that she'd been so generous and given over to what she was doing, he'd lost it completely.

The door latch clicked and he turned his head. She walked out of the powder room with her clothes and mask in place, but there was an adorable self-conscious flush on her exposed cheek and an even more exquisite glow of arousal coming off her like an aura. Her nipples were pencil tips beneath her second-skin jumpsuit, and the way she walked held the hip sway of the sexually aroused.

Unbelievably, he twitched back to life below his unbuckled belt. He instantly wanted to strip her and have her under him.

"I'm going to eat you alive," he warned her.

She shook her head. "I have to go."

"The hell you do." He'd tie her up if he had to.

"No, I do," she insisted.

"What happened?" He looked to the powder room, wondering what had changed between seconds ago and now.

"Nothing. I just… This was really nice, but I want to leave it like this. As a nice memory for both of us."

"We can keep the lights off," he blurted in a burst of panic.

"Ryzard, please." There were tears in her eyes. "Just this, okay?"

He swiped his hand down his face, unable to think where he'd gone wrong. *Why the hell was she shutting him out?*

"I won't force you to make love with me. You don't have to go." Hell, the last thing he was capable of right now was *talk,* but it would be better than her leaving.

"I know you wouldn't, but I want to. Thank you again."

She skittered a wide circle around him and slid through the cracked door.

She'd got him off and thanked him twice. *What the hell?*

Tiffany was still trembling when she slid between her sheets, both angry with herself and relieved. Maybe she should have stayed with him. Maybe this was her chance to get over her scars so she could pursue a relationship with another man in the future.

But she didn't want anyone else, and she didn't have the courage to expose herself to Ryzard.

With a moan of despair, she rolled onto her stomach and groaned into a pillow.

A muted bell sounded. She lifted her head and noticed a light flashing on the bedside phone. Picking it up, she said a wary, "Yes?"

"It's me. Where are you?"

His voice sent a race of erotic excitement through her veins and into her loins. "In my room, obviously," she said, unable to control the husky edge on her voice.

"In bed?"

"Sleeping, yes," she lied.

"Liar."

She rolled her eyes. *So* arrogant.

"What are you wearing?" he asked.

"Flannel jammies and a nightcap."

"Well, take them off, *draga.* I'm about to tell you what you missed by running out of here."

"You're going to force me to have phone sex?"

"Hang up any time."

"I might have enough without adding more," she murmured in a considering tone.

"Hmm? Oh. Clever," he said with dry amusement. "I never know what to expect from you, Tiffany. Although

I'm quite sure you're still aroused. Have you been thinking of how you nearly killed me tonight?"

"Did I?" She couldn't help smiling.

"So smug. Yes, you did. I didn't thank you, and I should have. You're a delightful lover."

She curled on her side so the phone was tucked under her ear. "Thank you for saying that."

"Are you naked yet? Because if my hands will not be stroking your gorgeous body, then I will listen as you do it."

"You wish." But she tingled at the thought. He was right about sexual excitement hovering under the surface. Her skin prickled to sharp life, making her feel sensual and deeply aware of all her erogenous zones.

"Satisfy my curiosity," he said in a low voice. "Are your nipples still hard?"

"It's dark, I can't see."

"Feel them."

She closed her eyes, tempted, but, "Ryzard, I meant it when I said we should leave it at tonight."

Silence.

Had he hung up on her?

"Are you still there?" she asked, hearing a forlorn note in her voice.

"At least tell me why you're cutting me off." Underlying the brisk frustration in his tone was an edge of something she'd heard this evening when he'd said, *It shows I belong.* She'd hurt him.

Through an aching throat, she managed to blurt out the worst cliché around. "It's not you, it's me. I'm the biggest head case going."

"You're concerned that I will be repulsed by these scars of yours."

"Yes," she admitted, breathing a little easier at his understanding.

"Why would that bother you if I was?"

"I— What?" Her whole body tensed. *Did* she disgust him?

"Why would you care about my opinion? Who am I to you? Just some stranger you slept with on a wild night, right?"

So many protests choked her, she couldn't speak. He wasn't just anyone, not after some of the conversations they'd had and the physical intimacies they'd shared, but she couldn't admit that to him. He was already way too close to sensing he meant more to her than their brief association should warrant. His opinion mattered a lot.

"You're expecting me to get naked, be as exposed as I possibly could be, and risk being rejected," she said in a strained voice. "Wouldn't that bother you?"

"It bothered the hell out of me when you walked out tonight. I was as naked as a man needs to be the first night." His anger blistered off the receiver, making her squinch her face in a cringe. "You've done it to me twice."

"I'm sorry." The words burned from all the way in the pit of her sick stomach. "I didn't look at it from your perspective. I wasn't rejecting you."

"You need to start looking beyond yourself, Tiffany."

"I just apologized. That doesn't happen often. I suggest you accept it."

He sighed with frustration, then said with austerity, "You have been dealt a cruel blow from life. I won't dismiss that. But it didn't kill you, so start learning to live with it."

Wow. He didn't pull any punches, did he?

"How?" she demanded in a burst of angry despair. "You're not telling me anything I don't know, but how do I just get over it?"

"You want to be with a man, Tiffany. You like it when I touch you. Be with me."

He did make her feel more confident, but it would take

about a hundred of these heart-to-hearts before she'd be able to face being naked in front of him.

"We could meet for breakfast," she offered. The inside of her cheek stung and she realized she was biting it, feeling very insecure at putting herself out even this much.

"Where?" he asked.

"I assume they have a buffet or a restaurant downstairs."

"I meant your place or mine, but I see. Yes, they have a breakfast room. Nine?"

He wasn't making any effort to hide his disappointment, but she only confirmed, "Downstairs at nine. It's a date."

Ending the call, she rolled onto her back and stared at the dark ceiling. What was she doing? There was even less point in seeing him at breakfast on their last morning. They'd never see each other again after that.

Still, just thinking about seeing him made her body feel ripe and wanton. Running her hands over the hard swells of her breasts with their taut tips poking sharply against her rippling fingertips, she tried to erase the sensations nagging at her. The hunger deepened, provoking memories of Ryzard leaning on the wall, disheveled pants barely containing flesh she had memorized with her mouth, his eyes heavy lidded and voracious.

Rolling a frustrated moan into her pillow, she wished she'd said yes to the phone sex.

When she arrived in the dining room, Ryzard was standing in the entrance talking to another woman.

It was a low blow and nearly made her turn in retreat, but he lifted his hawkish mask and held out a hand to her even before he locked his gaze on her.

Stupid watches. Hers was shivering at its nearness to his, just like her to him. As she walked across, she experienced a little thrill at how good he looked in simple black pants and a white shirt open at the throat. His hair, clipped so short you could barely tell it curled, was still damp.

A dip of insecurity accosted her at the same time. The woman gesturing so passionately in front of him wore a light cover-up over a bikini that barely contained her flawless figure. Her mask was equally spare, just a sleek line from temple to temple.

Tiffany felt overdressed in her pants suit and elaborate mask as well as intrusive as she arrived, causing the woman to break midsentence.

Ryzard grasped her hand in a firm, warm grip, drawing her a step closer while continuing to give his attention to the other woman. "Please continue."

"I—" She was obviously disconcerted by Tiffany's arrival. Her body language changed from enticing to standoffish. "I just wonder if the sudden rumors being spread about this weekend, talk of dirty deals and Greek Mafia connections, could be true. Zeus's reputation is important for all of us, and if he's no better than a crook we should talk about it. Figure out what to do."

Tiffany was a little lost, coming in late and distracted by the strength and heat of her *lover*. He smelled freshly showered, and his flimsy white shirt was hardly any barrier, allowing her to nearly taste the texture of his skin.

Still, being excluded niggled at her. She'd been The Family Behind Him too many times for her father, a required face in a photo, but heaven forbid she open her mouth. Being relegated to arm candy here, where she was supposed to be an equal, was the final straw.

"Who *is* Zeus?" Tiffany asked.

"No one knows," the woman said, dismissing her with a patronizing jerk of her shoulder, adding, "Which is part of the problem. He should identify himself so we can decide if we want to continue associating with him."

Tiffany followed the entreating glance the woman sent

to Ryzard. She was obviously trying to pull him over to her side for reasons other than any real concern about the club.

"That seems hypocritical, doesn't it?" Ryzard said calmly. "When we keep our own identities secret?"

"I have to agree. It's quite possible to have a wrong impression about someone until you know them better," Tiffany said with a significant look upward to Ryzard.

"Well, we don't keep any secrets from Zeus, do we?" the woman insisted. She wavered with indecision a moment as her gaze touched on his hand holding Tiffany's so possessively. Then she made a noise of impatience and muttered, "I'm just saying," before she walked away.

Tiffany raised her brows, not that Ryzard could see them and appreciate her pique at coming upon a woman hitting on him so blatantly.

"Good morning," he said before swooping to kiss her.

She stiffened, but he took his time, working swirls of reawakened passion down through her torso and into her belly until she softened into his loose embrace. When he lifted his head, he said, "I'm starving. You?"

Food was the last thing on her mind, but she followed him through the indoor/outdoor dining room to a table near the lagoon-shaped pool. They accepted coffee and placed their orders before she lost her ability to stay silent and asked, "Do you pick up women at all these things?"

Setting down his coffee, he regarded her with a hard look. "Your pretty blue eyes have gone quite emerald, *draga.*"

"Who is she?"

"That's a question I can't answer. Members do not out other members. That's why I didn't introduce you."

She narrowed her eyes. "If I had looked at my watch, would I have seen her nickname?"

He shrugged. "Possibly. Mine is turned off except for

you. She only spoke to me because we happened to meet at the door and have spoken before."

"About?" she prompted.

"It's confidential."

"Have you seen her away from these things?"

"Also confidential."

"So you won't tell me anything."

"This is how the club works. That's why it works. But I will tell you that I have never had a sexual relationship with her."

"And she would never admit to one if you had because members don't out other members. I'm just supposed to trust that you're telling me the truth."

"Yes," he said firmly. "I do expect you to trust me."

Her gaze dropped to the button he'd only half pushed through its hole in the middle of his chest.

"If you had let me make love to you last night, you would not be feeling so insecure this morning," he added.

Her heart skipped at that, but she only said, "I'm not insecure. I don't *know* you."

"Exactly."

Oh, he was infuriating. And sexy. Her eyes were eating up the way his shirt was perfectly tailored across the line of his shoulders and hugged the strength in his arms. Her fingers itched to unbutton the whole shirt and expose his very promising chest again.

It's just hormones, she tried to insist to herself, not wanting to succumb to feelings that were a lot more complex than mere lust.

"I'm jealous of her for being pretty," she admitted in an undertone, ashamed that she was this shallow, but, "I used to be and it gave me confidence. Don't deny that being physically attractive is powerful," she warned with a point of her finger. "My mother still turns heads and uses it every day. And she places so much importance on looks."

The weight of that knowledge slumped her into her chair.

"Sometimes I wonder if that's why she chose Dad and not Paul Sr. He wasn't ugly by any stretch, but Dad's got that Mr. President, all-American look. Mom wanted the best-looking kids in the state and she got them. Now, when she looks at me…"

Time to shut up. Her throat was closing and it was impossible to fix.

"Your mother sounds very superficial." His tone of quiet observation told her he'd heard and weighed every word she'd said. Being such a tight focus of his concentration made her feel oddly vulnerable and safe at the same time. It made her think he genuinely cared about what she was revealing.

"She's the wife of a politician. Her world revolves around how things look. You're judged on everything in that position. Looks matter."

"I suppose," he allowed with a negligent tilt of his head. "Did she push your father into politics?"

"No, it was something he wanted, but maybe that's the real reason she married him." Tiffany considered her parents' marriage a moment. "Dad is a good father, a super husband, a really good man, but he aspires to be a Great Man and Mom aspires to be the wife of one. She set me up to…" want? demand? "expect the same thing."

"Was your husband planning to go into politics?"

"If our parents had anything to do with it, yes." She curled her mouth in mild distaste.

"You didn't want him to."

Once again she was able to speak a truth to him that she couldn't say aloud to anyone else.

"I honestly didn't think I had a choice. But I've seen how that life has affected my mother over the years. Every word she says is guarded. Half the time she's Dad's mistress. His work is his wife. Our family day at the fair was always a photo op with Dad glad-handing everyone except us. He couldn't buy me the candy floss I wanted. A taffy apple was a better message." She sighed, still more bewildered than bitter. "My life was staged to look like the life I wanted, but we weren't allowed to actually live it that way."

"Another reason why I will never marry. Too much sacrifice on a family's part."

"Another' reason? You don't intend to marry? Don't you want children? That's the one thing I looked forward to when I agreed to marry. I wanted to give my kids the childhood I hadn't had."

As the words left her mouth, she realized how leading they sounded. As if this was a conflict they'd have to resolve before proceeding with their relationship. She never talked this openly, except maybe to her therapist, but who else did she talk to these days? She was out of practice with hiding her real thoughts and feelings.

"You can still have a family," he said with a calm blink of his eyes within the holes of his mask. "Why couldn't you?"

Behind her own mask, she burned with self-consciousness, her gaze fixed to his. Her finding that kind of happiness wasn't as easy as he made it sound, and he knew it. With her teeth bared in a nonsmile, she said, "Why don't you want to marry?"

"I'm married to my country," he stated. "As you said, my work is my wife. Everything I do, I do for my people."

She tried to ignore the dull pain that lodged in her chest. That was good, wasn't it? She admired patriotism, and that certainly kept things simple between them. No false expectations.

"How did you become, um, president?" she asked, faltering because it was an impulsive question that sounded a lot more loaded than she'd meant it to.

"I was elected," he said coolly.

She waited while their meals were delivered, then said, "I meant, how did people come to know who you are and want to vote for you? I'm sure it was covered in the news, but as you've said, that's usually slanted, and quite frankly I've had other things on my mind for the last few years. I missed how it all happened. I'm really asking what drew you back to your country and into representing it."

"My mother was killed in a random attack. I went back for the funeral and my father was determined to fight. I couldn't leave him to it. I was angry with myself for not returning sooner, for thinking someone else would sort out the trouble and I could return when there was peace."

"You're either part of the solution, or part of the problem," Tiffany murmured. "I'm sorry about your mom." Was that whom he'd been talking about yesterday, she wondered, when he'd held her in shared grief? "At least your father is safe."

"He died, as well. Fighting."

"Oh. I'm so sorry."

He waved that away with a lift of two fingers. "I believe he wanted it that way. To be with my mother."

"Still…" She swallowed, ready to cry for him because he seemed so withdrawn and contained. Tears would never dare to seep from his bleak eyes. "I'm sure he would be very proud of you for what you've achieved."

"Once you've paid the price of a loved one, you don't stop until the job is done. I managed to bring enough of our various factions together to throw over our corrupt government and campaigned on a promise of peace. There is still a very long road. The biggest challenge is keeping the country from falling back into fighting, but we had some corruption charges work through the courts recently that gave people confidence. Small things like that matter."

She nodded, tipping a little further into the primordial

world of deeper feelings for him. Genuine admiration. Awe. Empathy.

Careful, Tiffany.

"Shall we take the art walk?" he asked when they finished eating.

"I didn't know they had one." She looked around, expecting artists with pads and a jumble of still lifes and caricatures had arrived to line the stones near the pool.

"They set it up inside to avoid sun and humidity damage."

"Really? What are we talking about? Priceless artifacts? Da Vinci?"

"If something like that is on the market, absolutely. Most of it is contemporary, but they're all good investments."

Moments later, they entered a gallery of comic book art competing with old-world landscapes and elegantly carved wooden giraffes. She fell in love with a stained glass umbrella, mostly because it was so ridiculously useless.

"How much is it?" she demanded, searching for a tag.

"The auction is in a few hours."

"We'll come back?"

"If you like."

"I want to use it as a parasol against the sun." It had to weigh fifty pounds. It was the most impractical object ever created and she *had* to own it.

"You have a beautiful laugh," he remarked, tugging her into a space behind a giant sculpture of ladies' shoes. "I'd like to see you smiling under this umbrella of yours, your face painted by the colored glass. I'd like to see you sunbathe naked under it," he added in a deeper tone that seemed to stroke beneath her skin and leave a tingle.

At the same time his words put a pang in her heart. She wished...

He bent to kiss her, pulling her into his aroused body as if they were the only two people in the room. A second later, as his tongue invaded her mouth, she forgot everything except the feel of him, shoulders to thighs, branding her.

"I want you in my bed," he told her huskily, as he found her bare earlobe and drew it between his lips.

Her body felt as if it swelled to fill his arms, breasts aching, all her skin thin and sensitized. Willpower and self-protection fell away as she confided in a whisper, "I want that, too."

He lifted his head. His possessive hands stilled and firmed on her. "Yes?"

Her heart stalled. He wouldn't accept any more waffling. She swallowed, still terrified by the idea of being naked in front of him, but she would hate herself forever if she refused him out of sheer cowardice. With breath held, she gave an abbreviated nod.

His smile should have alarmed her. It bordered on grim, but a light of excitement behind his eyes made her tremble with anticipation. He really did want her.

Blood rushed in her ears so she barely heard him speak to a *petite q* as they made their way back to the main floor.

"Early checkout?" she repeated as he led her through the door the *petite q* released with a thumbprint and security override card.

"Gold membership has its privileges," he said drily. "But they'll only let me leave early. They won't allow us back in."

"Oh, but what about my things—?" She paused on the ramp down to the marina, where several eye-popping luxury yachts bobbed like toys in a bathtub.

"Our luggage would be packed for us regardless. That's the level of service we pay for, Tiffany." He waved and called something in Bregnovian to a young man as they approached a catamaran. It was called the *Luiza* and had an orange sail wrapped around its single mast. The body was such a brilliant white she had to squint.

"We'll remain docked a few hours yet," Ryzard said in

answer to a question from his crewman. "Unless we have to move to let someone out." He nodded at the boat they'd traversed to reach this one. "Tell the captain we're aboard and will order lunch when we're ready, but we don't wish to be disturbed."

Tiffany blushed behind her mask, thinking Ryzard was making it incredibly obvious what they were about to do. He didn't seem concerned, however, as he led her through the interior salon of sleek curved lines, the colors a soothing mix of bone and earth tones. Panoramic windows slanted over the lounge and bar, bringing splashes of turquoise water and cerulean sky into the room. Bypassing a short staircase that led to an elevated pilothouse of some kind, he brought her down a half flight of steps into the master stateroom.

"This is amazing," she couldn't help blurt. No stranger to the finer things in life, she was awestruck by the simple elegance and understated masculinity in the surprisingly spacious room. Drawers and cupboards in blond teak lined the space below the windows that provided a one-eighty view. A door led to an exterior deck on this side and into a well-organized head on the other. One curved radius corner of the room was a scrupulously efficient work space, the other a rounded sofa that looked to a flat-screen television set into the wall offset from the bed.

The bed itself was a king-size statement of power, tall and stalwart, its linens almond colored with a bold chocolate stripe across the foot. She dragged her eyes away from it as she heard a whispery sound and the light changed.

Ryzard moved with deliberation to draw woven shades down into a clip, allowing filtered sunlight to penetrate, but giving them privacy.

Her stomach swooped and she put out her hand, not sure where to find purchase when the floor was dipping at the same time.

"I thought we'd go to a room in the club," she said, linking her hands before her to hide that she was trembling with nerves. And excitement.

He turned from the last window and brushed away his mask, tossing it aside. "As I said, I don't want to be interrupted."

By staff wanting to pack their belongings, she imagined he meant, but couldn't speak because he came close enough to remove her mask.

She stopped him.

"I've seen your face, Tiffany."

"I don't want you to see how scared I am."

He frowned. "Of me?"

"Your reaction."

He shook his head, dismissing her fear as he trailed light fingertips over her clothing, grazing the sides of her breasts and settling warm hands on her waist. "I'm afraid I'll hurt you again. I wish you'd warned me the other night. I wasn't nearly as gentle as I could have been."

"I know pain, Ryzard. That was nothing."

"It was something," he told her, pulling her close enough to brush his mouth against hers, not properly kissing her. Teasing. "I'll never forget it."

An odd expression spasmed across his face before he controlled it, as if he hadn't meant to admit that to her, but she drew in his confession like air, deeply affected, wanting to hold on to this special feeling he provoked in her. Everything in her yearned so badly to please him, and she was so sure she wouldn't.

Get it over with, she told herself. She had to let him see and judge and reject before she climbed too high in optimism and desire. A long fall from excitement to disgust would be more than she could bear. If she did it now, before they'd gone too far, she'd still be able to dress and trudge into the nearest town to phone her brother—the one she kept forgetting about.

For now, she had to gather her courage.

Gently removing Ryzard's hands from her waist, she took a step back. The mask seemed like a tiny bit of necessary protection so she kept it, reaching first for the single button that held her linen jacket closed.

Removing it exposed her arm, marbled in streaks of red and pink, some parts geometric patterns from the grafts, other edges random and white. Not looking at him, she opened her pants and stepped out of them. Her left leg was as bad as her arm, and the top of her good right thigh was peppered with rectangles where they'd taken skin to patch the bad. Her stomach had the same types of scars. She threw off her sleeveless silk top and stood there in her cherry red bra and underpants and gold gladiator sandals.

For the life of her, she couldn't lift her chin. Her eyes were glued to the floor, her mind full of the rugged road map her body had become. No ivory virgin here.

"You do know pain, Tiffany," he said quietly.

That brought her eyes up. He studied her gravely, all the way to her toes, and gradually climbed his gaze back to her face. Stepping closer, he touched her chin to bring her face up and looked into her eyes. His were somber, but glowing with something fierce.

"You humble me. I don't know if I could have fought through such a thing."

She had to bite her lips to keep them from trembling.

Gently he removed her mask and let it fall. She felt incredibly vulnerable, standing before him nearly naked when he was clothed.

"Do not be ashamed of your courage to survive."

She had wanted to be told she was pretty despite her scars, but what he said was better, filling her with an emotion she couldn't describe. Tipping into him, she hugged him tight.

And realized he was aroused. His hand swept her bare back down to where her thong exposed her naked cheek. With a purposeful clench of his fingers into the firm flesh, he tilted her hips into pressing where he grew harder by the second.

"You're turned on," she breathed in wonder.

"I've got you naked next to a bed. How the hell else would I react?"

That made her laugh, then she squealed as he picked her up and lightly tossed her onto the mattress. Coming up on her elbows, she accused, "Caveman."

"Believe it," he confirmed, yanking off his shirt and dropping it away. His pants came off with similar haste. "Off with the rest," he ordered, jerking his chin at her lingerie. "This time we're both naked."

He was, in record time, and pulled off her shoes without ceremony.

"Don't wreck them. I like those," she protested, pausing in finding the clip between her breasts to reach for the strap of her shoe.

"What about these?" he asked, hooking two fingers in her panties at her hip. "Special favorite? Because I'm out of patience." He snapped them.

"Oh!" Why his primitive act turned her on, she couldn't imagine, but the way he loomed over her, practically overwhelming her with his strength, gave her a thrill. Probably because she felt totally safe despite his resolute expression and proprietary touch. He was impatient, but not without discipline. He threw away her bra, but then he simply held her, his weight on one elbow as he studied her breasts.

"Does this hurt?" he asked, tracing where her scar licked like a flame up the side of her breast.

"I can barely feel anything. Just a bit of pressure. Nerve

damage. You know how your face feels after the dentist and the freezing is just starting to come out?"

"Good to know. I'll focus where you can feel it." He cupped her breast and flicked her nipple with his thumb.

The sensation was sharper than she anticipated, and she flinched.

"No?" he prompted.

"I— No, it's good, just really..." She blushed. This was surreal, lying in full light with a gorgeous man naked against her. Twin desires to curl into him and to stop and give herself time to take it in accosted her.

He lowered his head to lick, and her inner muscles clenched like a fist, tearing a sound of reaction out of her.

Almost experimentally, he switched to her other breast, teasing and making her shift restlessly. It felt incredible, but wasn't quite as intense as the other.

He moved to her left one again and another shot of extreme sensation went through her, flooding her loins with a heated rush of pleasure. She didn't know if her nerve endings were compensating for others nearby that had ceased to work, but the way his tongue toyed so delicately made her pinch her thighs together.

"That one is really sensitive," she panted, smoothing her hand over his short, thick hair and clutching at his shoulders, not sure if she wanted him to stop or take her over the edge.

"I can tell," he said with smoldering approval. Opening his mouth on her, he sucked delicately, nearly levitating her off the bed.

"Ryzard," she cried, knee bending and thighs opening as she tried to grasp more of him. With a growl, he slid down and bit softly at her inner thigh. "Do you know how many things I want to do to you?"

Moaning, she threw her arm over her eyes and surrendered. "Do anything. I love everything you do to me."

For a second he did nothing. She wondered if she'd done something wrong and started to drop her arm away. Then she felt his touch delicately parting her. His mouth. Pressing the back of her wrist against her open mouth, she muffled her throaty groan of abject joy. To be wanted like this, so deliciously ravished, brought tears of happiness to the seams of her closed eyes.

And *oh* that was nice. Pleasure coiled and built on itself through her middle, winding her into the sweetest tension. She wanted release and she wanted this to go on and on. Then he slid a testing finger in her, and she knew exactly what she wanted.

And told him.

"I can't wait, either," he said in a raw voice, as if the truth stunned him. In a sliding lunge across her, he nearly yanked the bedside drawer from its table and seconds later smoothed latex down his length.

When he pressed into her, she welcomed him with a gasp, nails tightening into his skin as he possessed her with ruthless care, slow and inexorable. Through her lashes, she watched him watching her and bit her lip, feeling deeply exposed, but moved by the intimacy at the same time.

"I can't believe I'm the only man who knows how amazing you are," he said gutturally, hands holding her head as he rocked side to side, settling deep inside her, sealing their connection.

Her body didn't feel like her own. She trembled in arousal, limbs both weak and strong, clinging to him. Her mouth offered itself, parting and begging for his.

With a tortured growl, Ryzard kissed her, thrusting his tongue into her, wanting more and more of her. All of her. Indelibly.

But that intense, deep possession couldn't be sustained forever. Eventually, he drew back enough for ecstasy to strum through him as her sheath stroked and clenched around him. She smelled incredible, felt even better, tasted like forbidden substances. He became animalistic, purely in his physical state, senses captured and held by this creature who entranced him. Nothing entered his vision except the expression of exquisite torture against the unique pattern on her face.

In a rare moment of unguarded openness, he removed his internal shields so he could fully absorb the pure, sweet light of her. His only thought was to fill her with the same all-encompassing rapture that held him in its grip.

She sobbed his name and he increased his tempo, reacting to her need and compelled to fulfill it. She met him thrust for thrust, their bodies so attuned they scaled the cliff together and soared into the abyss with perfect affinity. Clutching her tight under him, buried deep in her shivering depths, he let out a ragged cry of triumph as he gave in to pulse-pounding release.

CHAPTER SIX

RYZARD ROLLED AWAY, then settled on his back, his body brushing hers, but only incidentally. He wasn't embracing or meaning to touch her that Tiffany could tell.

She turned her head to see his profile was unreadable. Not displeased, but not…

Oh, she didn't know what she was looking for. A spear of inadequacy impaled her. While she had been caught up in their lovemaking, she'd been fine, but now she was back to being scared and self-conscious of her scars. She sat up.

"Don't go anywhere," he said, hand loosely cuffing her wrist.

Ha. Where could she go? They weren't allowed back into the club. *Hello, big brother, can you pick me up at the docks?*

Glancing over her shoulder, she tried to read his mood behind his heavy eyelids, but his spiky lashes made it impossible.

"You seem…" She didn't want to reveal how sensitive she was to disapproval right now. They might have been intimate in other ways before, but this was different. It wasn't just the physicality or revealing of her scars. She'd been incredibly uninhibited, exposing the very heart of herself.

"It's probably best if I go," she managed in a husky voice.

"I don't know what I seem, but I'm only trying to assimilate something that—" He breathed a word in his own language. She suspected it was a curse, but his tone was kind of awed and self-deprecating at the same time.

Facing forward, she closed her lids against a sudden sting, biting back an urge to beg him to continue what he'd almost said. It sounded as if he was as moved by their love-making as she was, which was balm to her tattered soul.

He released her wrist to stroke her lower back, making her lift her head from where she'd let it droop to rest on her knees.

"Are you okay?" he asked.

"Just trying not to act like a first-timer."

"This is unique for both of us."

She tried not to drink too deeply of that heady assessment. She was already falling for him in little ways and couldn't afford to become too enamored. This was merely an extension of their one-night stand.

"You keep condoms in the drawer by the bed," she pointed out. "I'm not that unique."

A beat of dark silence, then, "*I* never claimed to be a virgin."

She wanted to glare at him, but couldn't risk him seeing how hard it was for her to acknowledge his experience. Why? What right did she have to possessive feelings? She was lucky to be included in his special club at all.

"And this won't be the only bed I'll ever be in, so—hey!"

He had her on her back and under him before she realized he could move that fast.

"Here's a tip for someone new to this," he growled. "We don't discuss past and future lovers, particularly when we're still making love to each other."

She blinked in shock, heart hammering.

His aggression fell away to a baffled, tender caress that he smoothed along her good cheek. "Don't make me feel guilty for my life before I met you. How could I have known that what I thought was pleasure…" His expression clouded with a look of such angst, it made her heart hurt.

"It's just chemistry," she assured him, teetering inwardly against her own words even as she attempted to comfort him with them. The remark went directly against her girlish desire to hear that she was actually very special to him.

She held her breath, hoping against logic that he'd offer such a pledge.

"Exceptional chemistry," he agreed. His hungry gaze followed his hand as he caressed from her lips to her collarbone, across the damp underside of her breast and down to her hip where his thumb aligned to the crease at the top of her leg. "But you do understand this is simply an affair? It can't lead to anything permanent. I'm not the sort of life partner you're looking for."

His blunt statement fell between them like a metal wall, softened only by the expression of regret on his face.

"Glad you said it first," she said with a poignant smile, hoping it hid the way she tensed internally. She was as wary of certain fantasies as he was, but not nearly as adept at cutting her emotions out of her heart. "I told you what I think of being the woman behind the man. You're merely a guilty indulgence, like cheating on a diet."

His brow winged, indignant but amused. "Let's fatten you up then."

Ryzard gave up trying to work. They'd been sailing three hours already, so he had another word with his captain, then remained at the helm while his instructions were carried out. As the wind whipped his shirt through the open windows of the pilothouse, he once again congratulated himself on having the wisdom to switch from a single-hulled sailboat to the double construction of a cat. The three-sixty views and flexibility with anchorage were worth the ribbing he received from traditionalists.

Hell, if he had allowed his concentration to wander like this on his old schooner, they'd all be dead, but here he could indulge himself with recollecting every delicious minute of his day. He'd devoted several hours to learning each and every one of Tiffany's pleasure triggers, stimulating both of them as he expanded both of their educations in physical delight. Sweetest of all had been her generous straddling of him, broken voice asking for direction as she tugged him along her path to bliss.

They'd been like drunkards at that point, sheened in perspiration. Her eyes had been glassy, her pouted lips reddened by a thousand kisses. Her breasts had swayed with their undulations, her hips an instrument of torture he wielded on himself as he guided her with hands clamped tight in ownership.

He'd been sure he would die, it had been that good.

Rubbing his face, he dragged himself back to reality, yanking open his collar in search of a cool breeze to take his libido down a notch. They were flying over the waves, skipping at a light angle, demanding he pay attention, but all he could think was, how could he be this aroused again? She'd drained him dry. They'd collapsed into unconsciousness, utterly exhausted from making love.

He'd woken soon after, sweaty and thick with recovery, wanting her again.

When he'd shifted, she'd grumbled without opening her eyes, "Don't move. My hip hurts. I need to keep my leg propped."

He didn't doubt it. His joints had protested his rising from the bed, and he'd never crashed and burned in a roadster. He'd substituted a pillow under her thigh and watched her settle back into sleep before taking his insatiable libido for a cold shower in a spare cabin.

Then he'd made a decision he was still second-guessing, but it was done. She was his.

I love everything you do to me. The power of that statement unexpectedly exploded in his mind again, but that first bit, *I love...*

He scratched his chest where a sensation gathered like sweat trickling. The tickle was behind his breastbone, uncomfortable and impossible to erase. *It's just chemistry,* she'd said as he'd been reeling from a depth of pleasure he'd never experienced before.

He'd agreed with her, clinging to that simple explanation, but it was harder to blame chemistry when he'd found himself unable to wake her and send her on her way.

Why not? Why was his response to her, on every level, so much more intense than it had been with the woman he'd loved, the one he'd pledged to marry? He hated himself for it, but he couldn't deny it.

He and Luiza hadn't had the luxury of time and privacy to soak themselves in sexual intimacy, though. Their bond had been forged by shared secrets and ideals. She had loved him when he'd had no one else. Her vision had become his.

She'd died before her dream could become reality, but he was still striving to make it come true. There was no reason to suffer pangs of infidelity just because he wanted to play out an affair with a particular woman for a little longer than a weekend.

He clenched his hands on the wheel, telling himself that the fact Tiffany had been a virgin weighed into his decision to extend their association. No man wanted to be a woman's first and her worst. He owed her more time and consideration than the average jaded socialite.

And she happened to have a sexual appetite to match his own. He kept mistresses when it suited him for that very reason. This was still a temporary arrangement, and Tiffany understood that's all he ever intended to have with any woman. His heart belonged to Luiza. If he couldn't marry her, he wouldn't marry anyone.

Having relegated Tiffany to her rightful place in his mind, he was ready to see her again. He nodded at the first mate, and the young man swung the sail to catch more gust.

Tiffany was falling out of bed.

She woke with a cry and a start, arms splayed to orient herself on the mattress. The room glowed a brassy yellow, the bed was a wreck and her body felt as if she'd been thrown down a flight of stairs. She held very still, trying to come to grips with the odd feeling the boat was not just bobbing in its slip, but moving.

It was. They were at sail!

She'd been on sailboats, but unlike the sharp angle that resulted in stumbling around to grip her way across a deck, this catamaran was only a hair off level, allowing her to rush the window and snap up the blind. Yep. Not another boat in sight. Just a speck of land on the horizon and glittering waves in every other direction.

"What the hell, Ryzard?" she said aloud.

Glancing around for her clothes, she caught sight of herself and cringed. Her hair was naturally straight, and all that sweaty sex had weighed it down into a droopy haystack. The side of her breast felt raw where it had been abraded by stubble and when she turned her nose to her shoulder, she could swear she smelled Ryzard's unique scent on her skin.

An odd, sexy feeling overcame her, making her want to loll in bed and call him to her, but she gave herself a firm shake. Where the hell was he taking her?

A very quick shower later, she dressed in her pants and sleeveless top to go in search of him. She forced herself not to be so cowardly as to wear the mask, but she still peered around corners, avoiding his staff.

She found him lounging in the shade of the aft deck,

taking up all the cushions of the built-in sofa as he read his tablet and sipped a drink made with tomato juice. A stalk of celery rested against its salted rim. He set it down when she appeared.

"I thought a few sharp turns might shake you out of bed," he said.

"Are you familiar with the term *kidnapping?*"

"I have business in Cuba."

"You're taking me to Cuba?" She gave a wild look around. Nope, not one hint of assistance in sight.

"Much as I'd love to anchor somewhere private and shirk my responsibilities, I can't. My weekend was booked for *Q Virtus,* but now we'll have to carve out our time around other commitments."

"Commitments like the one I made to get on a plane with my brother two hours ago? He'll be frantic." Dumbfounded, she braced a hand on her forehead trying to gather her scattered wits enough to formulate a plan.

"My staff spoke to him when they collected your things."

"Your staff collected my things. And brought them here?" She pointed to the deck, so astounded she could barely form words. "After they informed my brother that I was carrying on with you?"

"They're discreet enough to simply say you're my guest. Naturally he needed to be told why you weren't meeting him as arranged. Why are you upset? Relax. I realize you avoid the sun, but you can enjoy the view from the shade. I have a masseuse aboard, if you need."

"Ryzard," she said with a ring of near hysteria in her tone. "You said we'd stay in dock."

"For a few hours. We did. You overslept."

"You should have woken me! Not said things to my brother. He doesn't need to know about this. No one does. It's nobody's business but mine!" She splayed a hand on the place in her chest where he was taking up way more room than he should. Where he was lodged very close to places no one was allowed to go.

"When you called me your dirty little secret, I didn't realize you meant it," he replied stiffly.

Oh, she would *not* feel guilty. Maybe she was overreacting, but he didn't realize what kind of firestorm he would have set off with her family. This was bad.

"You should have asked me," she insisted. "And let *me* talk to my brother. Is there some way I can contact him?" Panic gripped her.

"If your mobile doesn't work, ask the captain for the ship to shore." He still sounded stung, but dealing with Ryzard came second to smoothing things over with Christian. What would he think of her?

She'd left her mobile in her room at the club and found it in her purse in the cabin where her things had been unpacked. Not Ryzard's cabin, she noted, but a separate one— and why did that bother her? She was upset with him, not supposed to be mooning about what it meant if he set her up to sleep apart from him.

Keying her code into her phone, she saw that her brother had left her a dozen messages.

"What the *hell,* Tiff," were his first words when she reached him.

"I know." She closed her eyes. She really should have thought this through before dialing. She was just so frantic to undo what had been done. But how?

"How does something like this even happen?" he demanded.

His askance reaction crystallized the confused self-consciousness inside her, so she felt very fragile and very brittle all of a sudden. Ryzard, despite his assumptions and autocratic ways, was not the villain. The problem with her family knowing about their affair, she realized, was the impossible vision she was supposed to live up to.

"You're the expert on picking up women. You know how it works," she retorted. "He came on to me with a great line. I fell for it."

The door clicked and Ryzard entered in time to hear most of what she said.

She averted her gaze from his darkening expression, prickling as her brother said, "You're too smart for that."

"Am I? Maybe I'm weak and desperate. Maybe I'm grateful for attention from *any* man."

In her periphery, Ryzard's arms folded and he said in an ominous undertone, "Is that true?"

"I knew it. He's taking advantage of you."

She sucked in a jagged breath, more hurt than words could express, but it was the ugly truth they'd all been dancing around since her accident. She wasn't worth a man's attention.

She flashed a look of resentment at Ryzard, angry that he was witnessing her humiliation. At the same time, she wished he didn't look so thunderous. She was desperately in need of backup. Instead, he'd probably leave her on a sandbar somewhere, but that was almost better than sending her back to the bosom of her kin.

"Thanks, Chris," she choked. "Thanks for letting me know there's no way he could possibly be attracted to me. I'm some broken, awful thing that ceased to be valuable when I ceased to be perfect. Shame rains upon us and it's my fault. Has Mom taken to her room?"

A weighted pause. She didn't dare look at Ryzard.

"I didn't say that," Christian said quietly.

"But it's true! Tell me something. How many times have you stolen a weekend with someone? Hundreds," she quickly provided. "How many times have you had to answer for it? *None.* And I never worked up the nerve to even kiss another man because I had a reputation to uphold. Not just mine, but the entire family's. Paulie's even."

He swore. "Okay, I get it. You're entitled to a private life, but this isn't exactly the time, is it?" he seethed. "Or the man."

"You haven't told Mom and Dad, have you?"

"I didn't know what to think, Tiff! This isn't like you."

"When have I ever had a chance to be who I am?" she cried. "I've been Dad's daughter, Paulie's intended. The bride who wore bandages. For God's sake, I'm an adult. A married, *widowed* woman. I shouldn't have to defend myself like I've committed a federal crime."

"No, you're right, I'm sorry. Truly."

"How bad is it?" she asked, hanging her head, weighted by guilt despite all she'd just said. "Do I have to talk to them or better to wait?"

"They don't know what to think, either. But they don't want to see you get hurt in any way, ever again. Is this thing serious with Vrbancic?"

She glanced at Ryzard. He didn't look quite so much as if he wanted to wring her neck, but he had an air of imperative surrounding him. As if he didn't intend to wait much longer for her to give her attention back to him.

"Not, um, really," she murmured.

Christian's sharp sigh grated in her ear.

"Oh, I'm sorry, did I miss where you married everyone you ever slept with?" she railed.

"So it's gone that far."

He didn't have to take a tone like the septic was backed up!

"Goodbye, Chris. Tell Mom and Dad whatever you want." She stabbed the end button and threw her phone onto the bed. Then dropped a pillow on top of it for good measure. And added a punch that left a deep indent.

"I'd like to say I'm above caring what people think of me, but when my family judges me, it hurts." Her baleful gaze met one that didn't so much judge as measure.

"You knew they would disapprove. That's why you were upset."

"Not because it's you. They would have been scandalized no matter who I slept with. Although, I'm sure there's some shock value that they sent me to talk to you and here I am. As God is my witness, I'll never, ever tell my mother I didn't even see your face the first time, let alone know your name." She buried her hot face in her clammy hands, reacting to all that had happened since she'd woken so abruptly. "This isn't the way I usually behave, Ryzard. I can't blame them for being shocked."

"Be careful how much you hate your parents, *draga*. They're the only ones you have."

"You're going to judge me now?" She lifted her face in challenge.

"I'm only offering the benefit of my experience."

"You hated your parents?" She didn't believe it.

"I was angry with them for sending me away. Keeping me away from my home. It felt like a rejection."

He hadn't explained that part before. A pang struck at how lonely and discarded he must have felt.

Beneath the pillow, her phone burbled. Tiffany made a noise and started from the room, then said, "Actually, I want to change. It's too hot for long pants."

Ryzard closed the door, but remained in the room. Apparently he intended to watch. Hell. The man gave her goose bumps without making any effort at all.

Skimming past the one-shoulder and long-sleeved shirts and dresses, she pulled out a skimpy sundress she would have worn only in the privacy of her suite yesterday. It was patterned busily in neon pink and green and yellow, hopefully bright enough to draw attention from her equally busy skin patterns.

The scared mouse in her wanted to hide under layers, but a spunky, more daring part of her wanted to test whether she still held his interest.

Stripping unceremoniously, even dropping her bra, she shrugged her arms under the spaghetti straps and tugged it into place, then picked up the flared skirt in a little curtsy, spinning under the direction of his twirled finger.

"Adorable. Now come here."

"And risk making love on that telephone? Possibly landing on buttons that could have serious consequences? No. You promised me a meal and we skipped lunch."

"Yet I recall being very satisfied with everything I tasted," he mused, one hand on the door latch. The other caressed her bottom as she exited in front of him.

Her blood skipped in her arteries, and she was blushing hard as she led him outside to where a table was set and chilled wine was ready to be uncorked. The sun sat low on the horizon, ducking beneath the shade to strike off the silver and crystal.

Ryzard held a chair in a corner for her and asked for a filtered shade to be drawn.

"I'm sorry I was such a pill," she said contritely. "You took me by surprise with this." She indicated the extravagance of the cat. "I thought we'd part ways this afternoon and maybe I'd see you with someone else at a future *Q Virtus* event. This is better," she allowed, but met his gaze with a level one. "But I do have to work."

"Apology accepted. And I've already instructed my crew to set up a work space in the cabin where your things were unpacked. It should be completed by morning."

"They're going to work while I'm sleeping in there?" she asked, already anticipating his reply.

"You won't be in there, *draga*. And you won't be sleeping."

* * *

Ryzard flipped through his emails on his tablet while he waited for Tiffany to finish her call. They'd had a surprisingly productive morning, despite lazing in bed first thing. An easy, affectionate companionship had fallen between them after her rather explosive reaction to waking at sea yesterday.

He still chafed a little, recalling it, even though he now understood it to be her own baggage with her family that had caused her to push him away like that. His reaction, however, continued to niggle at him no matter how much he wanted to ignore it. Her claim that she was with him out of desperation had slapped him with a surprisingly sharp hand.

She was volatile. A woman as sexually passionate as she was would have strong feelings in every aspect of her life, he supposed. He could only imagine what kind of mama bear she'd be about her children.

Sucking in a breath at having taken such a bizarre turn in his mind, he lifted his head to see her set aside her phone.

"Done. Really sorry," she said.

"Don't apologize. We both have to work. I made you wait this morning."

She gave him a look that said, *Seriously?* and slid her eyes to the crewman setting out their air tanks.

He grinned, amused by her blushing over his referring to the way they'd been driving each other into a frenzy, fresh out of the shower, when he'd had to take a call that couldn't be put off. Afterward, they'd nearly ripped each other apart, and breakfast had been a quietly stunned affair when her bare foot atop his had pleased him well beyond what was reasonable.

They'd parted ways after, each moving to their separate work spaces, but he'd been distracted by her proximity. With most women, that would signal the end for him. Not with Tiffany. His brain couldn't even contemplate an end to this. It had barely started. She was too extraordinary.

Her phone rang and she turned from removing her wrap, clad only in her bikini as she stepped toward the table where she'd left the phone. "I don't have to get that. We'll pretend we're already in the water and— Oh shoot, it's my brother. I should answer. Why are you staring?" She followed his gaze to her torso, then sent an anxious look to the crewman who had lifted her tank, ready to strap it onto her.

"I'm staring because you're hot as hell," Ryzard prevaricated. "Take your call or you'll be wondering what he wanted."

Somewhat flustered, she stabbed the phone, then held the screen before her for the video call. "Hey," she said as she picked up her wrap and shrugged her arm into it.

Ryzard sighed inwardly. He hadn't meant to make her feel sensitive. He'd been looking at her scars, yes, but only thinking that a woman with less zeal for life would have succumbed to such injuries. Tiffany's ferocious spirit was the reason she'd survived, and he was very glad she had.

"You're naked?" Her brother frowned. "It's the middle of the day. I thought it would be safe to call."

"Excuse me, darling," Tiffany said to Ryzard. "My brother has called to ask if the sun is over the yardarm. Could you lift the sheet and see?"

Christian sputtered, Ryzard looked to the sky for patience and his crewman buried a snort of laughter into his shirt collar. Although Ryzard had to admit it was nice to know she gave others a hard time, not just him.

"We're about to go swimming, you idiot," she said to her brother. "See? Bathing suit." She ran her phone down her body as if she was scanning for radioactivity, showing him the strapless band and itsy slash of blue. Then she turned the phone to show him the equipment on the deck. "There are the breathing tanks and scuba flippers. There's the mask that's going to give me an anxiety attack so Ryzard will have to buddy-breathe me to the surface. Is my virtue restored? Want to tell me now why you called?"

"Dad hasn't come across anything useful yet, but said he'd ask around."

"Motivated, is he?" The way Tiffany's blond lashes lifted to send a resolute look toward Ryzard made his blood kick into higher gear. "Tell him I appreciate anything he's able to pass along."

"As do I," Ryzard told her as she hung up. "If you're talking about what I think you are."

"I asked Christian to put a bug in his ear. Dad's not speaking to me directly right now, but I don't know if that's because he's in Washington and doesn't have time for the kind of conversation he thinks we need to have or if he's genuinely angry. I hope you don't mind, but I was worried Dad might—" She shrugged apologetically. "I'm his little princess. I didn't want any grumpiness he felt toward you to come out with anyone in a position to affect your situation. If he knows I have an interest in the outcome, he'll take care to support your petition. Or at least not damage it."

His ears rang with the impact of what she was saying. "He has that kind of influence?" It wasn't like him to underestimate people, but his sexual enthrallment had temporarily shortened his sight of the bigger picture.

"He's very well connected. And I'm being overcautious," she assured him, moving to put a hand on his arm. "Don't worry. He wouldn't do anything rash. Something like throwing support behind a leader who hasn't been recognized… It's too big a gamble going into an election. If anything he'll be even more circumspect, couching his reaction while trying to find out everything he can. He's not going to stir up a lynch mob or anything."

"No shotgun wedding?" he prompted, throat dry. How far would her father go for his daughter's groom?

"Absolutely not," she assured him.

He should be relieved. He couldn't betray Luiza's memory by contemplating marriage to another woman, but in the back of his mind a voice whispered, *If it was for your country...*

He brushed the thought aside, trying to remind himself this was a simple fling. Two people enjoying sexual compatibility and the luxury of Caribbean waters. If he took a moment to reassess Tiffany, not just because she was lissome and golden, not simply because she had a quick, intelligent mind and a clear understanding of politics, but because she could soon be first daughter of the United States of America, that didn't mean he was being disloyal to his one true love. Luiza had had a dream for their country, and he was obligated to consider any avenue to achieve it. That's all he was doing.

He watched her frown at her diving mask, lips white where she pinched them together. She'd told him about her aversion to wearing things tight against her face, but he watched her draw in courage with a deep breath and wrestle the mask onto her face.

"I'm really worried I'll freak out down there," she said in a tone made nasal by the mask covering the upper half of her face. Her eyes behind the glass were anxious.

"You're tough," he told her, pride and regard moving in him. "You'll handle it."

"You don't know that." She set a hand on her bare chest. "My heart's going a mile a minute."

"But you're trying anyway, despite your anxiety. That's why I know you'll be fine," he assured her.

He quickly slipped into his own gear, not wanting to make her wait for the distraction of reef and shipwreck to take her mind off her fears. Holiday fun, he insisted to himself. Nothing so complex as wanting to coax her past bad memories because he felt compelled to share the wonder below the surface with her.

Why it mattered to him that she go with him was a puzzle he didn't study too closely. He could just as easily dive with one of his crew and had in the past, but he was aware of a preference for staying aboard with her over diving without her.

That wasn't like him. He was not a dependent person. Tiffany had been surprised the other day when he'd told her he didn't want a wife or children. He understood the reaction. Everyone in the world wanted a lifetime companion and offspring, but after Luiza, he'd closed himself off to the idea.

He *didn't* want emotional addiction to another being. It made a person vulnerable, and he couldn't afford such weaknesses.

But the thought of marrying Tiffany kept detonating in his mind, trailing thoughts of sleeping with her every night for the rest of his life.

It was because of the advantages she offered him. It would be a practical move, not something he did out of a need to connect himself irrevocably to her. He didn't want or need *family*.

He needed to stabilize his country and make good on his promise of peace.

"You look like a frog," she said as they readied to jump.

"So kiss me, Daddy's Little Princess. See what I turn into."

She did, quick and flirty, then bit her smile onto her mouthpiece and fell back into the water.

He leaped after her.

CHAPTER SEVEN

"THAT WAS FANTASTIC!" Tiffany panted, still breathless from their ascent from a shipwreck covered in coral and barnacles, populated with colorful fish darting in and out of fronds. Ryzard had carried a spotlight so the wash of blue-green from the filtered sunlight had disappeared, revealing the true brilliance below.

He handed off his tank to his crewman, then heaved himself to sit on the platform at the stern of the boat, legs dangling beside her. "Up?" He offered a hand.

"Still recovering. Give me a sec," she said breathlessly.

He relayed their gear as they both stripped, lifting her tank off her back, muscles flexing under the glistening latte of his tan. His black bathing suit was ridiculously miniscule, making American men such as her brother seem like absolute prudes with their baggy trunks. She'd heard people refer to those teensy tight suits as banana hammocks and budgie smugglers, but on the right man, they were sexy as hell.

A crooked finger came under her chin, and he lifted her face to look him in the eye. Beneath the water, his foot snaked out to catch her at the waist and guide her into the space between his knees.

"What?" she challenged, hands splaying on the steely muscles of his flexing thighs.

"Are we staying in the water a little longer?" he asked suggestively. "You can't look at me like that and not provoke a response."

She flicked her gaze downward and saw he'd filled out the tight black fabric to near bursting.

"Don't ever let anyone tell you you're not beautiful, *draga*. When you smile, you light up the room, and when you're aroused, I can't take my eyes off you."

The water should have bubbled and fizzed around her, she grew so hot and flushed with joy.

"Will you come to Bregnovia with me?"

Oh. It was an out-of-the-blue question with huge implications, the most important being, *he wanted to keep her with him.*

Surging upward, she straightened her arms and let her chest plaster into his, meeting his hot kiss with open-mouthed, passionate joy.

"Yes," she agreed.

One big hand came up to cradle the back of her head and the other dug into her waist, holding her steady while his calves pinched her thighs, bracing her in the awkward position. Their kiss went on for a long time, sumptuous and thorough.

With a tight sound of frustration, he jerked back. "No condom," he muttered.

"What? There's plenty of room in that suit for one."

"Not much room at all, actually," he growled. "You'll take the lead into the cabin."

Laughing unreservedly, she let him pull her the rest of the way out of the water and onto his lap. "At least we know what you turned into down there."

He raised his brows in query.

She whispered, "Horny toad."

He pinched her bottom as he urged her inside.

* * *

The landscape from the airport was one of a country in recovery. When her brother had said Bregnovia could use their firm's expertise, he hadn't been kidding. They left the partially bombed-out tarmac, wound past a scorched vineyard and turned away from one end of a shattered bridge that spanned a canyon to zigzag into the riverbed, where they four-wheeled over a makeshift crossing before climbing the hairpin curves on the far side to enter a city that looked like a child had kicked over his blocks.

But what a city it had been. Bregnovia's capital, Gizela, was a medieval fairy tale on a river that, until dammed for electricity and irrigation, had been a trading arm in and out of the Black Sea. Low canals still lapped at the stone walls in its village square. Beyond that quaint center, stark communist housing stood next to even more modern shopping malls, but nothing escaped the wounds of recent war. Rubble punctuated in a small landslide off a facade here, crooked fencing kept children out of a teetering building there.

Fascinated by the contrast of beauty and battle, Tiffany barely spoke until they drove through gates that were twelve feet high and thirty-six feet wide. Their ornate wrought-iron grillwork with gold filigree appeared startlingly new and grand.

"This is your home? It looks like Buckingham Palace."

"It is a palace," Ryzard confirmed casually. "Built as the dacha for a Russian prince during tsarist times. The communists spared it—a KGB general appropriated it—but it was the last stand for my predecessor. We're still repairing it from the siege. It's only mine while I'm president, but I'm paying for the refurbishment, as my legacy."

Despite the bullet holes and the pile of broken stones that might have once been a carriage house, the palace made the White House look like a neglected summer cottage, especially with its expansive flower bed that formed a carpet beneath a bronze statue of a woman with an arm across her breast, the other outstretched in supplication—

Tiffany read the nameplate as the limo circled it. Inexplicably, her heart invaded her throat, pulsing there like a hammered thumb. *Luiza*.

Ryzard had said she was his country's martyr, revered like their Lady Liberty, but this statue wasn't staid. It didn't project a state of peace and optimism with a torch to light the way forward. It was anguished and emotional and raised all the hairs on her body. This statue wasn't a symbol or an ideal. She was a real person.

Whose name was tattooed on Ryzard's chest.

Not wanting to believe the suspicion flirting around the periphery of her consciousness, Tiffany left the car and walked inside to confront an oil portrait of the same woman in the spacious drawing room. Here, Luiza's serene smile was as exquisite as Mona Lisa's, only eclipsed by her flawless beauty.

Again it didn't seem like a commemorative pose that a country hung in the National Gallery. There was a wistful quality to the painting. It was the kind of thing someone lovingly commissioned to enshrine a memory.

Luiza's eyes seemed to follow Tiffany as she accepted introductions to Ryzard's staff. Thankfully they quickly left her behind as Ryzard and his porters took her up the stairs and along the colonnaded walk that circled the grand entrance below and brought her to a place he called the Garden Suite.

"It's the only one in the guest wing that's habitable," he said with a minor twist of apology across his lips. "But your work space is here." He left the bedroom and crossed the hall to push through a pair of double doors into a sitting room that had been tricked out with office equipment and a replica desk that Marie Antoinette would have used if she had run a modern international construction firm. "You won't have any problem working outside your country? With the different time zone?"

"We're global and I've been working from the family mansion. The advantage to living like a recluse is that no one will expect me to show up in pers— My umbrella!" The stained glass piece hung at a cocked angle in front of the window, just high enough for her to stand under it. "You said we slept through the auction," she accused.

"I placed a reserve bid before we left."

Moving in a slow twirl, she closed her eyes and imagined she could feel the colors as they caressed her face. "You're spoiling me."

"I want you to be happy. You will be?"

She opened her eyes to the window and the back of Luiza's bronzed head beyond the glass. Her floating spirits fell like a block of lead. She couldn't shake the feeling that Ryzard had a statue of his old girlfriend on the lawn.

"Tiffany?" he queried, voice coming closer.

"Where will you be?" she asked, leaving the window and leading him back across the hall to the bedroom. Here, at least, the windows faced the river.

"Too damned far away," he replied.

"Why? Security? No outsiders in the president's bedroom?" she guessed.

"Certain customs remain quaintly adhered to."

"Mmm." She pushed her mouth to the side, hiding that she was actually quite devastated. "I don't suppose our president could get away with bringing women home, either." The porter had gone so she jerked her chin at the door, saying, "See if that door locks."

"Subtle," he said drily, "but I can't."

"I don't know what you think I'm suggesting," she challenged, tossing her head to cover up that she rather desperately needed to reconnect physically. The emotional hit of what looked quite literally like a monumental devotion to Luiza shook her tenuous confidence. Badly. Now he was rejecting her, inciting a quiet panic. "I only meant that if I'll be sleeping alone, I need to feel safe."

"You won't be alone."

"I can have a guard with me?"

"That would be detrimental to the state of peace I'm trying to maintain," he stated with one of his untamed smiles. "No, I will sleep with you, but right now I have to go outside and salute my flag. It's a custom I observe when I return after being away. People gather to see it. It reassures them of my commitment. Would you do me the favor of putting on something suitable and joining me? They'll be curious."

Here we go again, she thought with an unexpected face-plant into dread.

I bet Luiza would do it, a taunting voice sang in follow-up.

"Problem?" he asked, obviously reading something of her reluctance.

"Just disappointed we can't test the bed," she prevaricated.

"They stand at the gate, if you're worried they'll see you close up."

"It's fine," she assured him.

It was. When she stood outside thirty minutes later, face shaded by a hat from the surprisingly hot sun, her entire being swelled with admiration as she watched Ryzard in his presidential garb stand tall and make a pledge to his flag. He wasn't a man going through the motions. His motives were pure, his heart one hundred percent dedicated.

With tears brimming her eyes, she watched him step away from the flag with a bow, taking his respectful leave. Then he turned and saluted the statue of Luiza, first pressing the flats of his fingertips to his mouth then offering the kiss to her in an earnest lift of his palm.

Tiffany stood very still, fighting not to gasp at the slice of pain that went through her. It wasn't the gesture that struck her so much as the anguish on Ryzard's face.

Her suspicions were confirmed. He loved Luiza, really loved her as a strong man loves his soul mate. His pain was so tangible, she could taste its metallic flavor on her tongue.

She reached out instinctively, longing to comfort him, but he stiffened under her touch, catching her hand and gently but firmly removing it from his sleeve.

"When I asked about your tattoo, you never said—"

"I know," he cut in, releasing her and taking one step away. "It's difficult to talk about."

"Of course," she managed, curling her fingers into a fist even though the blood was draining from her head, making her feel faint. Would she have come here if she'd known? The starkness of his rejection felt so final she could barely stand it. "I'm so sorry."

She meant she was sorry for overstepping, but he heard it as a lame platitude and dismissed it with an agitated jerk of his shoulder.

"I never want to go through anything like it again. To love like that and lose— Never again," he choked, flashing her a look that was both adamant and apprehensive.

He quickly looked away, but that glimpse of his resolve struck like a blow. She knew what it meant: he would never *allow* himself to love again. It would make him too vulnerable.

Making another quarter turn, he bowed his head toward the gates.

That's when Tiffany noticed the crowd of fifty or sixty people with faces pressed through the uprights of the gate, witnessing his rebuff and her humiliation. They didn't applaud, didn't wave, just stared at them for a few moments before slowly beginning to disperse.

Even they seemed to know she had no place here.

As she followed Ryzard back into the palace, she couldn't tell if Luiza's portrait met her with a smug smile, or a pitying eye. Thankfully, they both had work to catch up on. She needed space, even one situated with a prime view of Luiza's last haircut.

Oh, don't be bitter, Tiffany.

Ha, she laughed at herself. Bitterness had been her stock in trade after the pain of her recovery had receded from blinding to merely unrelenting. She really had believed her life was over, but Ryzard had shown her she could have a measure of happiness.

She considered the boundaries of her happiness later, as she soaked in a tub of bubbles. Ryzard had had to take a call, leaving her to dine alone, and she felt very much as her mother must have for much of her marriage. Not so much slighted as resigned. This was the reality of living with someone in his position. If he had loved her, the sacrifice might be worth it, but he didn't.

His heart belonged to Luiza. Indelibly.

A tiny draft flickered the candles in the corner of the tub and sudden awareness made her glance toward the door, then sit up in a startled rush of water and crackling bubbles.

Ryzard slouched his shoulder against the frame, arms folded, hip cocked. The most decadently wicked glint of admiration gave his shadowed expression a sexy cast.

She'd set a stage for him if he chose to come looking for her. A delicate lily-of-the-valley scent hovered in the humid air and a low-volume saxophone hummed sensuously from the music player. That hadn't prepared her for the impact of his tousled hair, wrinkled collar under a pullover sweater, or the way her heart leaped when he reached to tug his sweater over his head.

"I came to sneak you down to my room, but you've made me an offer I can't refuse. Before I forget, though…" He leaned over her, one broad hand cradling her chin while he crushed her mouth in a hard, thorough kiss that made her murmur in surprised delight.

"You were in danger of forgetting to do that, were you?" she asked breathlessly as he straightened to take off his shirt and kick away his pants.

"An undersecretary from your State Department called. It's not a promise to vote in favor, but it's a promising sign they're leaning that way."

"Oh!" The impulsive clap of her hands sent bubbles exploding like flakes off a snowball. "That's wonderful."

"That's thanks to you." He eased into place behind her, his muscular body buoying hers as he pressed her to relax back into him.

"I didn't do anything."

"I'm sure it was your father's influence at play."

"Mmm." She let her head loll against his shoulder, absently playing with his fingers where he roped his forearm across her collarbone. Her brow pleated. She wanted him to be happy, wanted peace for his country—who wouldn't wish peace for everyone in the world? But a pang sat in her chest. She wished something more personal had brought him to her this evening.

"It's a very big step," he said, drifting his hand down the slippery slope of her breast. "Do you know how many countries hesitate to make a move because they fear instigating something with yours? If America supports us, the other two-thirds of the votes I need would fall into place fairly quickly. I know I said I wouldn't force any dress-up on you, but there may be a few state dinners in our future."

She bit back a huffing laugh. *So* not surprised.

Just say no, Tiffany.

But refusing to play her part meant refusing this relationship. Despite it's misty future, she wasn't ready for it to end.

Especially when Ryzard lightly toyed with her nipple, making her murmur approval and slide against him. Was he manipulating her with her own responses, she wondered distantly? He was hardening against her, so he *did* want her.

Still, she hated herself a little for being so weak and easily managed. If she couldn't have the same effect on him, she at least wanted to break through his control. Rolling over, she grasped him in a firm hold, the way she'd learned he liked, and nipped his bottom lip.

He jerked his head back. The gold flecks in his green eyes glinted like sparks off a sword. "It's like that, is it?" he growled.

She grinned and sent a small tsunami across the ledge as she dragged herself onto her knees and straddled his thighs. As she kissed him with all the passion releasing inside her, she used her whole body to caress him, wiggling her hips to encourage the palms that shaped her backside.

Licking into his mouth, she reached to caress his thick erection again and started to take him into her.

"*Draga,* wait," he rasped against her open mouth. "Protection." He leaned away to reach for his pants.

Inhaling anguish along with a small dose of shame, she wondered what she had been thinking, offering unprotected sex. Was she that desperate for something permanent with him?

"Actually, let's go to the bed," he said, pulling away to leave the tub and let water sluice off him onto the floor. "It'll be more comfortable." He reached to draw her onto her feet, then lifted her out, carrying her wet and dripping into her bedroom, where he followed her onto the bed.

She bit him again as he tried to kiss her.

"What has got into you?" he asked, pulling her scratching nails off him and pinning them above her head in one hand.

"Not you," she taunted, inciting him with the arch of her body into his. "What's taking so long?"

With a bite of the packet and a stroke of a finger and

thumb, he was covered and pushing into her, not rough, but not gentle. Inexorable. She was ready, but not entirely. The friction caused her to draw in a breath of both surprise and anticipation.

"Better?" he asked, holding himself so deep inside her, she released a little sob. He eased back. "Tiffany, what's wrong?"

She shook her head. "Just make love to me."

Ryzard did, because he couldn't be with her like this and not thrust and withdraw and savor and bask. But he held out, making it last a long time for both of them, sensing a wall that needed prolonged lovemaking to erode. He blamed himself for the distance. He was struggling with having her here. It had been an impulse to ask her and he didn't regret it, but he was still having a hard time adjusting.

For the moment, however, he closed his mind to his inner conflicts and opened himself to Tiffany.

She writhed beneath him, so beautiful in her struggle to resist the little death of orgasm, clinging to him as she hung on to their connection. It couldn't last forever, though. Nothing could. His heart stopped. The whole world did. Ecstasy overtook them and nothing existed for him except her.

He stayed in that trance for hours, trying to sate their appetite for each other with repeated joinings. The wall between them receded and he didn't worry about it again until the next morning, when she woke in his bed.

She glanced around with the perplexed befuddlement of the bubbleheaded blonde he sometimes teasingly called her. "Where am I?"

"The Presidential Bedroom," he answered, shrugging into his suit jacket while he enjoyed the show.

The sheet slipped as she sat up. Her blue eyes blinked and she smoothed a hand over her tangled hair. "Why?"

"Your bed was wet," he reasoned, distantly aware that wasn't the whole truth. He had wanted her in here before he'd ever gone looking for her, but he was distracted by the shadow that passed behind her clear-sky irises as she looked around.

"Problem?"

She only lifted the sheet and glanced at her naked body. "Please tell me you put clothes on me when you carried me here."

"You were awfully heavy. I couldn't manage another ounce."

Her baleful gaze held a dire warning that made him grin. He picked up her robe from the chair and tossed it to the foot of the bed in answer.

She stood to pull it on, not returning his smile. The niggling sense of being held off returned full force.

"Are you all right, *draga?*" he asked, moving forward to cup her cheek and force her to look up at him.

She didn't quite meet his eyes, only saying with an ironic twist to her mouth, "Let's just say it's a good thing I had a warm bath to loosen my muscles before we played for gold in that triathlon last night."

"Shall I rub you down?" he offered, stroking a hand down her back in concern. He was ready to insist, wanting the physical connection to her even if it wasn't a sexual one. The way she stayed resistant to his touch bothered him.

"I thought it was verboten for me to be in here? I'll be fine. I'll have a hot shower and do my stretches." She kissed him, but it was a minimal brush of her lips against the corner of his mouth before she disappeared.

He frowned as he crossed to pick up his phone from the nightstand. Absently he straightened the snapshot of him and Luiza on horseback, wondering if he was imagining the wedge between him and Tiffany.

It was probably for the best if there was one, he reasoned. This was an affair. They couldn't afford to develop deeper feelings.

Still, he left his room with a pain cleaved into his chest.

CHAPTER EIGHT

TIFFANY TRIED TO ignore the fact that Ryzard was in love with a dead woman and soak up what he offered her: generous lovemaking and a boost to her confidence.

On his catamaran, she'd quit trying to hide herself from his crew. Three days in Bregnovia and she was even more comfortable in her own skin. He kept threatening to take her along on his public appearances and she always managed to talk him out of it, but part of her longed to go on a date the way they had at *Q Virtus*.

Pressing a strapless dress in sunset colors to her front, she decided to have a pretend date with him tonight. She imagined that like all men he had a thing for short skirts and low necklines. She'd knock his socks off.

An hour later, she'd run the straightening iron over her hair to give it a sheen and applied a final layer of glossy pink to her lips, making them look pouty and ripe. The dress offered her breasts in half cups, hugged her waist and clung so tightly across her hips she could barely walk. The gladiator sandals didn't help, but man did she look hot. The fact her scars were fully revealed by the itty-bitty dress didn't faze her.

She paused to consider that. A light coat of concealer downplayed the mottled scar on her face, but she wasn't about to smear her whole body with the stuff. Ryzard wouldn't notice or care either way. He thought she was gorgeous exactly as she was. It was such a painfully sweet knowledge, she had to stop and cradle it and blink hard or ruin her carefully applied makeup.

Digging her nails into her palms, she focused on the sting to clear her head, aware she was dangerously close to tumbling into love with him. It was because he was her first, she reasoned. He was gorgeous and smart and *so* patient with her moodiness and baggage. He commanded everything around him with calm ease, and that would make anyone feel safe and protected and cherished.

The real tell would be when they separated. She couldn't hide from her parents forever. The one stilted conversation with her mother had centered on exactly how long she intended to be away.

Tiffany hadn't wanted to admit she was afraid to leave. Would Ryzard miss her if she went home for a week? Or would it be the end of their associations?

She shook her head, having learned to be present in a moment, especially if it lacked pain. No one had a crystal ball telling what would come next. For now, she and Ryzard were together and happy.

With a calming breath, she searched him out in his office. He was watching his favorite newscaster and remained behind his desktop screen as she entered, head bent in concentration as he listened, expression grim and contained.

"What's happening in the world to make you look so severe?" she teased as she sidled up to him. "A beautiful woman just walked in. Whatever you're watching, forget it and notice *me*."

His arm came around her waist, grasping her close and tight, but his other hand caught hers before she could press his head down for the kiss she wanted. The look in his eyes was not easily interpreted, and the voice beside her startled her out of trying.

"Should we continue this later?" the newscaster asked.

"No," Ryzard answered.

Tiffany cried out in surprise and jerked against Ryzard's arm, but he held on to her without laughing.

"I thought you were watching a broadcast," she gasped, covering her heart.

The familiar face on the screen gave a tight smile of acknowledgment.

"I didn't realize I was walking into a video call. I apologize. Oh, gosh," she realized with a belated hand going to the bad side of her face. "I can't imagine what you think of me, making an entrance like that."

"I was already aware you two were close," the talking head said. He was a globally known face, one who'd elevated from foreign-correspondence stories to hard-hitting investigative stories and in-depth analyses of world politics.

At the moment she didn't have much choice with regard to how close she was to Ryzard. His arm was like a belt of iron, pinning her to his side, his tension starting to penetrate as she read zero amusement in his expression over her mistake.

"What's wrong?" she asked, instinctively bracing herself.

"We had company after our dive," he replied.

"Paparazzi?" She tried to step back, but he kept a tight grip on her.

"It doesn't matter, Tiffany."

"Of course it matters! Otherwise your friend here wouldn't be calling to warn you. Is it photos or video?"

"Photos." Ryzard fairly spat the word.

"The photographer knew I would never touch something purely to incite sensation," the newscaster said. "So they didn't offer them to me or I would have kept them off the market completely. Instead I heard about it secondhand and I've suggested a countermeasure to draw attention from their release."

"What kind of countermeasure? What are they saying?" She looked between the screen and Ryzard, panic creeping into her bloodstream.

"They don't sell clicks by being kind," Ryzard said brutally. "We'll meet in Rome," he told his friend on the screen. "You're right that a face-to-face broadcast interview will have more impact than something thrown together remotely."

"I'm not going on camera!" Tiffany cried.

"No," Ryzard agreed with the full impact of his dictatorial personality. "But you'll accompany me to the interview—"

She shook her head, growing manic. Part of her wanted to explode in rebellion, the other desperately needed to crawl away and hide.

"I need to go home." Had her father heard yet? She struggled against Ryzard's steely grip, then froze, thinking of her mother's reaction. "My family will be livid. They're already barely speaking to me—"

"Calm down." He thanked his friend and promised to be in touch with his travel arrangements, then turned off the screen. "The sun will still rise tomorrow, Tiffany. No one has died."

"It would be better if I had. That's what they'll be thinking."

"Don't talk like that. Ever." He gripped her arms and gave her a little shake.

She quit struggling, but kept a firm hand of resistance against his chest. "We're not one of these families who has a disgrace every minute, Ryzard. My accident was the worst thing Dad has ever had to field with the press. Given it was more tragedy than scandal, it didn't do him any harm in the polls, but it was still a monumental circus. He won't appreciate this."

The look of wild outrage Ryzard savaged over her made

her shrink in his hold. "Your father enjoyed some kind of political *benefit* from your near death?"

"He didn't mean to! I'm just saying that's how it works. Chris and I know that. We don't go off and sleep with people who are shaking up the maps of an atlas, putting the UN on notice, then get ourselves photographed for the gossip rags so Dad has to make explanations for our behavior. This, what you and I are doing, has to stop. I have to go home." She tried again to push away.

"So you can be shunned and cloistered? No," he gritted through his teeth, holding her in place. "The photographer is the villain here, not you. Not us."

"I'm still about to be vilified, aren't I? And I don't want…" Her voice wavered. Her muscles ached where she still held him off. "Home is my safe place, Ryzard. I'd rather be there when— How bad are they? The photographs, I mean."

"Don't think about them," he commanded. "You'll never see them if I have anything to do with it." His voice sent a wash of ice from her heart to her toes, it was so grim. "But I can't allow you to be away from me when they're released. They'll say I've rejected you, and that's not true. Besides, it doesn't sound as if your family will support you, so no, you stay with me."

She drooped her head. "They would support me," she insisted heavily. "The wagons get circled at times like this. And after it blows over, they would still be there for me. They do love me. It's just complicated."

"I will *ensure* it blows over," he said, forcing her chin up and looking down his nose from an arrogant angle, but his touch on her gentled even if his voice didn't. "You're coming to Rome with me, Tiffany."

She held back from pointing out she was perfectly capable of booking a charter flight and getting herself anywhere she darned well wanted to go. If he was only being authoritarian, she probably would have, but he sounded concerned. He sounded as if her feelings mattered, not just his image. That softened all the spikes of umbrage holding her stiff, making her shudder in surrender.

"Okay," she acquiesced.

"Good girl."

"Don't push it," she warned, but turned her face toward the caress of his fingertips as he smoothed her hair back behind her ear. Her eyes drifted closed.

"I'd like your father's contact number."

"Oh, no, I'll call Dad." She straightened, but found herself still in the prison of his hold.

"No, Tiffany. This is my fault. I should have taken more care to shield you. He's already uncomfortable with our relationship. I should have introduced myself before something like this made our first conversation an unpleasant one."

"I really think—"

"We're not negotiating, *draga*. We'll stand here until you've given me his number, but I'd like to get to Rome sooner than later, so make this easier on both of us."

"You're unbelievable," she choked.

"His people will have questions about the arrangements I've made. Quit being stubborn," he pressed.

Her? Stubborn? Kettle. *Black.*

With a sigh of defeat, because she really didn't want to face down her father *and his people,* she offered up his private mobile number.

How could he kiss something so hideous?

She didn't know why she looked it up. She should have known better, but she'd been compelled to know what they were saying. It was horrid. Beyond cruel.

Ryzard had been furious when he had emerged from

his shower and found her with his tablet in her lap, fingers white, throat dry, eyes unable to meet his.

"Why would you take a dose of poison? It's self-destructive, completely against everything you are," he'd growled, nipping the tablet away from her and tossing it across the room onto the bed.

Somewhere in his words she supposed a compliment lurked, but all she heard was disapproval. It made her cringe all the more.

The flight to Rome was exhausting and silent, his mood foul, but she hadn't wanted to speak, either. She didn't want him to notice her. She seemed like a burden, something he was carrying with him because he had to, not because he wanted her. How could he want anything to do with her when she was bringing shame on him like this?

Like sleeping with snakeskin. She shuddered at the headlines and comments from trolls that would stay in her mind forever. *Her husband was lucky he died and didn't have to stay married to that.*

Ryzard's interview was staged in a hotel room, the pristine white decor too bright for her gritty, bloodshot eyes. Neither of them had slept despite lying next to each other for a few hours. He'd stroked her for a time, but she hadn't been able to respond, too frozen inside. Feeling betrayed. Her parents hadn't called, not even replying to her text that she was available if they wanted to talk. The only friend she had right now was Ryzard, and he was so remote he might as well have stayed in Bregnovia and sent a wax double in his place.

She'd been too afraid to ask what he intended to say and wound up standing at the side of the room, staring dumbly from the shadows into the light as he took his seat. The interview began.

Her father had done a million of these things, so she wasn't surprised to hear them tiptoe through a variety of political tulips on the way to the meat of the interview. Ryzard's devotion to his country was on full display, and she imagined the whole world was reevaluating him as he spoke passionately about Bregnovia's desire for peace and plans for prosperity. She hoped so. He deserved to be taken seriously.

She grew more and more tense as the interview dragged on, however. Didn't they realize the audience was waiting for the mention of her name?

Twenty-five minutes in, the question finally came.

"Photos have circulated showing you with American heiress Tiffany Davis. Is it serious?"

"I take very seriously that your bottom-feeder colleagues are making their fortune on photos that for all we know have been manipulated for a higher profit."

Nice of him to defend her with such an implication, but the photos had not been airbrushed. She genuinely looked that bad.

The interviewer smiled tightly. "I meant is the relationship serious?"

"That's between us. We're private people," Ryzard stated implacably.

Tiffany caught back a harsh laugh. Did he really think he'd get away with as little as that?

"My sources tell me you met at the notoriously secret *Q Virtus*," the newscaster continued.

See? she wanted to cry. The press never rested until they drew as much blood as possible, even when they called themselves a friend.

"That's true," Ryzard allowed.

"*Q Virtus* is a rather exclusive club, isn't it? What can you tell me about it?" the journalist pressed.

"I'm sure contacting them would get you more information than you'd ever get out of me," Ryzard said smoothly.

Oh. Ha. That was smart. She relaxed under a ripple of

humor. The public's insatiable curiosity would now turn to the club. Papers could trot out as many before-and-after photos of Tiffany Davis as they wanted, but viewers and readers would be more interested in learning the names of other people in the secret club. They'd hungrily eat up the scant yet salacious details of what went on there. She and Ryzard would be old news before the credits rolled on this broadcast.

In fact, when she watched later that evening, she noted that while the names rolled, her own image came forward to Ryzard's reaching hand. She shook hands with the newscaster and thanked him, all of them standing in friendly banter. Her good side was angled to the camera. Her hair was done and her makeup was decent. Wearing a simple alabaster suit, she looked...normal. Pretty even.

Ryzard clicked it off as it went to commercial. She collapsed on the foot of the hotel bed, emotionally exhausted. Could it really be over as easily as that?

Ryzard watched Tiffany as he unknotted his tie and released first the cuffs, then the front buttons of his shirt. As tough as she was, he'd seen what a toll this attack had had on her. She'd been shutting him out as a result, and that infuriated him. Her talk of running away where he couldn't reach her had nearly put him out of his mind.

He was still beside himself that this incident had happened at all. His captain had warned him that an unidentified boat kept turning up in their radar, but he'd shrugged it off. None of his mistresses in the past had warranted much attention, but he supposed his own profile was elevated to the international stage these days. Tiffany's family was certainly of a level to feed the appetite of her country's gossip columns.

And she's not just a mistress, is she? The question beat in warning like a jungle drum in his chest, ominous and dark.

His plans for his relationship with Tiffany were changing, but he hadn't wanted to allude to anything more in his interview. The last time his link to a woman had been public and indelible, she'd been used as a pawn in his country's civil war and the outcome was fatal.

Seeing Tiffany beaten and wounded by words shook loose his nightmare of losing Luiza. He'd grasped at anger to counter his resurgence of helplessness, hating that he couldn't stem the damage being done to her, but agony and guilt were constant. He should have protected her better. If he could have stopped Tiffany from searching out what they were saying about her, he would have. Humanity's capacity for ugliness astounded him. His job, the one he'd taken on for his country, for his own sanity, was to push brutality and attacks to the furthest fringes of existence that he could.

And keep himself apart so the pain of life couldn't reach inside him and wring him into anguish.

It wasn't easy when Tiffany sat with her spine slouched and her golden hair trailing loose from its neat bun, seeming incredibly delicate, like a dragonfly that had its wings crushed. When she was like this, she stirred things in him that needed to stay in firmer places. The chin-up, spoiled and cheeky Tiffany he could easily compartmentalize as a friendly partner in a game of sexual sport. Like a tennis opponent who gave him a run for his money, athletic and quick.

The vulnerable Tiffany frightened him. She made him feel so ferociously protective he would do violence if he ever found the photographer who'd reduced her image to a commodity in filthy commerce.

Shaken by the depth of his feelings, he tried to pull them both out of the tailspin with a blunt, "Dinner out or in?"

She sighed and looked up at him. Her heartrending expression was both anguished and amused. His heart began to pound in visceral reaction, and he swayed as though struck with vertigo, not sure why.

"My first thought is, *Duh, Ryzard.* Of course I'd never dine in public, but how could I be such a coward when you've just defended me so fiercely? No one else has. I can't tell you how much that means to me."

A sensation of wind rushing around him lifted all the hairs on his naked chest, as if he was free-falling into space. Her gaze was so defenseless, he couldn't look away. She reached inside him with that look, catching at things he couldn't even acknowledge.

"You already know I would only wish away your scars because I hate that you were hurt at all. But I see them as a badge of your ability to overcome," he heard himself admit. "Your sort of willpower, your deep survival instinct, is rare, Tiffany. You probably don't realize it because it's such an integral part of your nature to fight, but not everyone accepts such a life blow and makes herself live through it."

Luiza hadn't, he acknowledged with a crash of his heart into his toes. Thinking about her when he was with Tiffany, contrasting them, was wrong. Setting aside Luiza in his mind was like ripping an essential part of him away and abandoning it, but he had to do it. They couldn't occupy the same place inside him, and right now Tiffany needed him.

"All my life I heard, 'You're so pretty.' Like that was the most important thing to be. You're the first person to compliment me on having substance. I really thought I'd lost everything by losing my looks."

Where Luiza had built him into the man he was with vision and belief in him, Tiffany slayed him with honesty and vulnerability. His heart felt as though it beat outside his chest. When she rose and came to him, and went on tiptoe to brush soft lips against his jaw, he closed his eyes in paralyzed ecstasy. Deep down, at a base level, it felt wrong to be this gripped by her, but he couldn't help it. In this moment, she was all he knew.

"Thank you for wanting me exactly as I am."

He did. God help him, he wanted her in ways he couldn't even describe.

They shouldn't come together like this, with hearts agape and defenses on the floor, but he couldn't *not* touch her. Pulling her in, he settled his mouth on hers, tender and sweet. The animal in him wanted to ravish, but the man in him needed to cherish.

She drew an emotive breath and kissed him back in a way that flooded him with aching tenderness. The sexual need was there, strong as ever, but it sprang from a deeper place inside him. Hell, he thought. Hell and hell. Lingering feelings of infidelity fell away. This woman was the one he had to be faithful to. *This one.*

The rending sensation inside him hurt so much he had to squeeze her into him to stop what broke open, fearing his lifeblood would leak away if he didn't have her pressed to the wound. Her arms went around his neck, light palms cradling the back of his skull as she fingered through his hair, soothing and treasuring and filling the cavernous spaces in him with something new and golden and as unique as she was.

When they stripped and eased onto the bed and came together, it was with a shaken breath from him and a gasp of awe from her. She gloried in his possession, and he bent his head to her breast in veneration, golden lamplight burning the vision of her into his memory with the eternity of a primordial being caught in amber.

Twin fingers traced on each side of her scar, the sensation dull on one side, sweet on the other. She stretched in supreme pleasure and reached for him without opening her eyes, finding only cool, empty sheets where he was supposed to be.

"I'm already showered and dressed, *draga,*" he said on her other side. "You said to let you sleep and I did as long as I could, but we have to leave soon. We have a dinner engagement in Zurich."

"Are you serious?" She rolled onto her back so she could see him where he stood over her, his knife-sharp suit of charcoal over a dove gray shirt set off with a subdued navy tie. He looked way too buttoned-down, hair still damp, chin shiny and probably tasting spicy and lickable. She skimmed the sheet away and invited, "Come back to bed."

"Your parents are expecting us. I already agreed to see them, but if you'd like to send our regrets…"

"They're in Zurich?" She sat up, bringing the sheet to her collarbone as if her father had just walked in the room. "How? Why?"

"I left it to our collective staff to work out the how. I simply extended the invitation when I informed him about the photos. He wanted you to come back to America. I said you were accompanying me to Rome and that I had a commitment in Switzerland, but that we'd be pleased if they could meet us there."

"How delightfully neutral. I guess that explains why they haven't been in touch. They've been traveling." She threw off the sheet and walked naked to find her phone, pleased at the way he pivoted to watch her.

Sending him a saucy smile over her shoulder, she clicked her screen and tapped in her code, reading aloud the message she found. "'Staying with the deHavillands in Berne.' That's the American ambassador. Mom went to school with her. Longtime friends of the family. 'Where will you be staying?'" She looked to him.

"At the hotel where the banquet will be held. My people should have sent the details already. I'll ask them to extend the invitation to include your parents' friends." He reached inside his jacket pocket for his mobile.

Tiffany heard only one word and lowered her phone, barely hanging on to it with limp fingers as she repeated, "Banquet?"

He gave her a long, steady look. "Something I arranged months ago. I've been trying to ease you into the public eye, *draga*. Don't look so shocked. It's not something I can miss since it's a charity I personally fund. We remove land mines and petition to stop their use completely. They're an appalling weapon."

She felt as though she stood on one, but he didn't coddle her over what attending would mean. Given everything that had happened, she supposed it was time to set aside her fear of being in public. As long as she had him by her side, she'd be okay, wouldn't she?

CHAPTER NINE

A FEW HOURS LATER, she wasn't so sure. She'd taken an *in for a penny, in for a pound* approach and forgone the one-shouldered gowns that would have disguised a lot of her scarring, deciding instead to let her freak flag fly. Her halter-style gown set off her breasts and hips beautifully and was the most gorgeous shade of Persian blue that glistened and slithered over her skin as she walked.

...snakeskin...

Stop it. She pretended she was her old self, the somewhat infamous fashionista who had graced more than her share of best-dressed lists. With her trained yoga posture reaching her crown to the ceiling, shoulders pinned back with pride, she entered the lounge and took the druglike hit that was Ryzard in a tuxedo.

"I knew you wouldn't disappoint me," he said. His smile was sexy and smug, but held a warmth of underlying approval.

Winded, she dissembled by checking her pocketbook, trying to grasp hold of herself as she reacted to him and the effect he had on her. Did he know how defenseless she was around him? She suspected he did. He was coming to know her very well, maybe too well. There was an imbalance there because he could see right past her defenses, but he remained unpredictable to her.

As if to prove it, he came forward and threaded a bracelet up her marred arm until it wrapped in delicate scrolls against her biceps. It was a stunning piece of extravagant ivy tendrils fashioned from platinum. Diamonds were inset as random pops of sparkling dew, fixating the eye.

"It's beautiful."

"When people stare, you can say, 'Ryzard gave it to me. He thinks I'm a spoiled brat, but wouldn't change a thing about me.'"

She wanted to grin and be dismissive, but she was too moved. Her voice husked when she admitted, "You do spoil me. I have no idea why."

"You inspire me," he confided, then swooped to set a kiss against the corner of her mouth. "Lipstick, I know," he muttered before she could pull away in protest. "In the future, don't put it on until I've finished kissing you."

"Then we'd never leave the room, would we?"

"And how is this a problem?" He held the door as he spoke, the light in his eye making her laugh, reassuring her the evening would turn out fine.

They stopped by another suite on their way downstairs. He'd arranged it for her parents and the ambassador. Her father greeted her with a long hug before he set her back. Then he looked between her and Ryzard, not seeming to know where to start.

She quickly introduced them and included the ambassador's husband, Dr. deHavilland, using Ryzard's title as the president of Bregnovia, and heard the crack in her voice as she queried, "Mom didn't come?"

"The ladies are fussing down the hall," the doctor said after kissing her cheeks. Taking her chin, he turned her face to eye her scar. "The specialist did wonders, didn't he? It's good to see you out, Tiffany. Ryzard, what's your poison? We're having whiskey sours."

He accepted one and she squeezed his arm. "Do you mind if I...?"

"Of course, go say hello, but we need to be in the ballroom to greet the guests in fifteen minutes."

"Five," she promised with a splayed hand and hurried in search of her mother, nervous of the confrontation, but experiencing the homesick need to reconnect.

Following voices through a bedroom to the open door of a bathroom, she approached and set her hand on the inner door only to hear a makeup compact click over her mother's voice. "Are we supposed to believe he's in love with her? Any fool can see he's using her for our connections."

"Any fool except me?" Tiffany blurted, pushing the door farther in while outrage washed over her. It was followed by a stab of hurt so deep she could barely see.

Nevertheless, her vision filled with the flawless image of her mother turning from the mirror. Shock paled her mother's elegantly powdered cheeks. An automatic defense rose to part her painted lips, but first she had to draw a breath of shock as her gaze traveled her daughter's appearance and measured the amount of exposure. A trembling little head shake told Tiffany what her mother thought of this gown.

"You won't be comfortable in that."

"You mean *you* won't," Tiffany volleyed back and turned to leave. A type of daughterly need for her mother's bosom had driven her in here, and now she wished Barbara Holbrook had stayed home.

"Tiffany Ann." The strident voice didn't need volume to stop Tiffany in her tracks. "He told your father he wanted to marry you. You met him last *week*. What are we supposed to think?"

Tiffany spun back, thrown by the statement. "He did not."

Her mother held her lady-of-the-manor pose, the one that had too much dignity to descend into a did-so, did-not quibbling match. Instead, she gave Tiffany another once-over and asked primly, "How on earth did you come to be his guest? I mean, if he had brought a party aboard, I'd understand you being swept along, but obviously he wants us to believe he has a romantic interest in you. What sort of promises has he made you?"

Tiffany heard the strange lilt in her mother's voice. Concern, but something else. Something shaken and protective...

She felt her eyes go wider and sting with dryness as understanding penetrated. Her mother genuinely believed she was being used—and was too blind to see it.

If her high school diary had been passed around the football locker room, she couldn't have felt more as though her deepest feelings were being abused. If only she could have defended Ryzard. If only she believed he had deeper feelings for her beyond the physical and amusement with her "great personality."

God, maybe he didn't even feel that much for her. Maybe it *was* all about who her father was. Insecurity nearly drove her to her knees, but she made herself stand proud and state what she'd let herself believe.

"He hasn't made any promises. He wants me for my body. It's mutual."

Dumbly she turned and walked out, floored by what her mother had said about Ryzard wanting to marry her. Was it true? Because if it was, her mother was right. It wouldn't be love driving his interest in her. They *had* met only ten days ago.

She tried to swallow away the painful lump of confusion that lodged itself high behind her breastbone.

Ryzard set down his drink as she appeared and held out his crooked arm. "Ready? We'll see you downstairs," he said to the men.

"Tiffany," the ambassador scolded, following her with a

swish of skirts. "You can't speak to your mother like that. She's been telling me how worried she's been for you, not just because you dropped out of sight with a stranger—I apologize if that sounds rude," she added in an aside to Ryzard. "But since—"

"I *know*. The accident. I've been a great burden on them, but can you understand how sick I am of having that define me? I'm better now. It's time for both her and Dad to butt out of my life."

She yearned for everyone to leave her alone so she could lick her wounds in private. It pained her horribly that everyone could see how weakly she'd fallen for this incredibly handsome, indulgent charlatan who had soothed her broken ego and wormed his way toward her heart. All in the name of advancing his own agenda.

"Where is this rebellion coming from?" her father clipped in his sternest tone. "You were never like this before. Your mother and I can't fathom what's got into you. Letting you go to work has obviously put too much stress on you."

"*Letting* me." She jerked up her chastised head, filling with outrage.

Beside her, Ryzard took her good arm in a warm, calming grip. "If you'll pardon an outsider's observation? Every child has to leave the nest at some point, even one who was blown back in and needed you very badly for a time. Your daughter is an adult. She can make her own decisions."

Despite that statement of her independence, she found herself letting him make the decision for both of them to leave. A crazy part of her even rationalized that even if he *was* using her, he was also helping her find the state of autonomy she longed for.

As they waited for the elevator, a jagged sigh escaped her. "I can't do this, Ryzard."

She meant the banquet, the evening, but he misunderstood.

"Don't let this upset you. Listen, I visited Bregnovia after finishing university. I could have stayed. My mother wanted me to, but I chose to drift across Europe like pollen in the wind. I was making a statement. They had forced me to leave as a child, but they couldn't make me stay as an adult."

"And now you hate yourself for not spending time with them. You think I should go back and apologize?" She looked back down the hall, hating the discord with her family even as she dreaded facing them again.

The elevator car arrived and Ryzard guided her into it.

"I don't hate myself as much as I should. Everyone does need to leave the nest at some point, *draga.* But be assured that your parents are operating from a place of love. Your father had some very pointed questions for me. He is the quintessential father who feels a strong need to protect his baby girl."

With bloodless fingers clinging to her pocketbook, she lifted her gaze to meet his. "Did you tell him you want to marry me?" Her voice sounded flayed and dead, even more listless than the tone she had used to discuss her prospective marriage to Paulie.

Surprise flashed across his expression before he shuttered it into a neutral poker face. "He asked me about my intentions when I called. I said they were honorable. What else could I say?"

"You told me this relationship wouldn't lead to anything permanent. When did you decide it could?"

He turned his head away, profile hard with undisguised impatience, then looked back, fairly knocking her over with the impact. "What are you really asking, *draga?*"

The car stopped and she swayed, stomach dipping and clawing for a settled state. "You weren't ever going to marry, but then you realized exactly how useful my father could be. Is that right?"

"Yes." No apology, just hardened, chiseled features that were so remote and handsome she wanted to cry.

"We talked about how much I enjoy being used, Ryzard."

The doors of the elevator opened. His handlers were waiting, one reaching to hold the door for them.

"We need a moment," he clipped.

"No, we don't." Her voice was strangled, but she stepped from the elevator into the bubble that was its own bizarrely familiar shield against reality. Her skin burned under the stares of his people, but she allowed only Ryzard to see how much that tortured her as she turned to glare up at him. "If this is what I'm here for, then let's do it. I'm probably better on stage than you are. Smile. Nothing matters except how this looks."

"Tiffany," he growled.

Arranging the sort of warm, gracious smile her mother had patented, she sidled beyond his reach and asked a handler, "Where would you like me to stand in relation to the president?"

Talk about land mines. Ryzard felt as though he stood in a field of them as he welcomed his guests and waited for the misstep that would cause Tiffany to discharge. She was the epitome of class though, greeting people warmly as he introduced her, maintaining a level of poise that made his heart swell with pride even as his blood ran like acid in his veins.

We talked about how much I enjoy being used.

He struggled to hide how much his conscience twisted under that. Did she think he couldn't see what this evening was costing her? He was so deeply attuned to her that he felt her tension like a high-pitched noise humming inside his consciousness, keeping him on high alert. It was fear, he realized with a *thunk* of dread-filled self-assessment. She would run given an opportunity, and that kept him so fixated on her he could hardly breathe, braced as he was to catch her before her first step.

He ought to let her go if that's what she really wanted, but he couldn't bear it when she hadn't even given him a chance to explain. The way she'd thrown her accusation at him in the elevator had been a shock. He'd answered honestly out of instinct, because any sort of subterfuge between them was abhorrent to him.

But distance was equally repugnant to him, and she was keeping an emotional one that didn't bode well for sifting through things he'd barely made sense of himself.

As for her pithy suggestion that all he cared about was his image, she was dead wrong there. He cared about her. Thinking about how much he cared made him feel as though the elevator's cable had been cut and he was still plummeting into the unknown.

They didn't have a chance to speak freely again until they were dancing after dinner. He kept his gaze off her, dangerously close to becoming aroused from holding her. Every primordial instinct in him wanted to drag her into the nearest alcove and stamp her as his own. The way they moved perfectly together no matter what they did seduced him unfailingly.

"Another one bites the dust," she murmured.

"What does that mean?" he asked with a flash of his glance into furious eyes that scored him with disdain.

"You can't keep your eyes off my mother. I told you she was beautiful."

He realized he'd been staring at the distraction of white hair swept in a graceful frame around aristocratic bone structure. Mrs. Holbrook's blue eyes stood out like glittering sapphires on the sateen of flawless skin as she watched them. Where Tiffany had a seductively full bottom lip, her mother's was narrow and prim, but that hint of severity lent her countenance keen intelligence. She was the height of elegance when she smiled and scrupulously well-mannered. She had thanked him warmly for inviting them even as her gaze consigned him to hell.

"She's not the one giving me a hard-on, *draga*. She's keeping it from becoming obvious. I'm in danger of catching pneumonia from her glare. I take it she doesn't approve of our affair?"

"I thought we were engaged." Limpid eyes, as capable of beaming frost as her mother's, glared up at him.

He involuntarily tightened his hands on her. "Not here, Tiffany. Not now."

She snorted, lashes quivering in a flinch, but it was her only betrayal of how much his deferral stung. He silently cursed, realizing he was forcing the taffy apple upon her.

"We'll talk upstairs as soon as I can get away," he promised.

"Mom and Dad are going back to Berne with the deHavillands first thing in the morning. They want me to come, so it would probably be better if I stayed with them—"

"Like hell," he said through his teeth. She was so stiff in his arms, he thought she'd shatter if he held her too tightly, but the idea she'd leave him made everything in him clench with possessiveness.

She showed him her good cheek, the skin stretched taut across it. Her voice wavered. "You were so appalled at the idea that Dad would use my accident for his own gain, but the minute you saw an advantage to your own precious country, you—"

"Enough," he seared quietly through gritted teeth. "Marriage is not something I take lightly. Even thinking of marrying you is the breaking of a vow I made to myself and a dead woman. You have no idea what it costs me."

With a little gasp, she stopped moving, forcing him to

halt his own feet. He looked down at her, as appalled by what he'd revealed as she seemed to be.

"Luiza," she stated under her breath, lips white.

He flinched. Hearing her say his beloved's name was a shock.

"Da," he agreed, nudging her back into dancing, feeling cold.

The air of thick tension surrounding them threatened to suffocate Tiffany, but she was a trained pony. The dance continued and her company smile stayed in place while all she could think about was the snippets of information he'd revealed about his tattoo, his lady liberty, his marriage to his *country*.

The rest of their waltz passed in a blur of tuxedos and jewel-colored gowns, glittering chandeliers and tinkling laughter. When he returned her to their table, her parents rose with their friends, ready to take their leave.

"Goodbye, Ryz—" she began.

"Don't even think it," he overrode her tightly.

"I have a headache," she lied flatly. "I'd like to leave."

"Then we will," he said with equal shortness. "Let me inform my team while you say good-night to your parents."

Seconds later he cut her from the herd and whisked her up to their suite.

"You're not making friends behaving like this, you know," she whirled to state as he closed the door behind them. "My father won't have your back in any arena if you continue to kidnap his daughter."

"I know your father hates my guts, but you will not let him separate us. If you're angry with me, then you stand here and tell me so," he railed with surprising vehemence, yanking off his tuxedo jacket to throw it aside. "Do not put yourself out of my reach. That is the one thing I will not tolerate."

Deep emotion swirled from his words at hurricane force, buffeting her. She unconsciously braced her footing, absorbing his statement with a wobble of her heart in her chest that left all the hair standing up on her body. It wasn't fear exactly. More of a visceral response to his revelation of intense feeling. Her body was warning her not to take his outburst lightly. He was startlingly raw right now, and anything but taking great care with how she reacted would be stupid and possibly hurtful to both of them.

She could hurt him.

A reflexive shake of her head tried to deny the thought. His face was lined with grief, emotions he felt for someone else, but a glint of something else in the stark, defensive gaze stilled her. A strange calm settled in her mind despite the racking pain of being used still gripping her.

The suspicion he feared being wounded by her was so stunning, she could only stand there hugging herself, not knowing what to say.

She had to say or do something. His hurting destroyed her. It was particularly intolerable because it had its roots in his love for another woman, but as much as she wanted to sublimate that knowledge, a masochistic part of her had to know the details. It was like assessing an injury so she'd know how to treat it.

"Was…" She cleared her throat. "Will you tell me about her?"

He turned away to the wet bar. Glass clinked as he poured a drink, drained it, then refilled his glass and poured one for her. When he brought hers across to her, his face was schooled into something remote while his eyes blazed with suppressed, but explosive emotion.

"Were you married?" she asked in a strained whisper. *Did you love her?* She couldn't bring herself to ask it.

"Engaged. She wanted to focus on winning the war, not planning a wedding. She was a protestor, an idealist, but very passionate and smart. I met her when I came back for my mother's funeral. I was beside myself, ready to seek retribution, but Luiza helped me develop a vision that people would rally behind. She was the velvet glove to my iron fist."

"You said she was your country's icon. That everyone revered her. What happened?"

He brought his glass to his lips, took a generous swallow then hissed, "She was captured and would have been used against me. She took herself out of the equation."

Appalled horror had her sucking in a pained breath, one she held inside her with a slap of her hand across her mouth. *Once you have paid the price of a loved one, you do not stop until the job is done.*

She stared at Ryzard over her hand, brutally aware there were no words to compensate for what he'd just told her. She didn't need the details. The horrifying end was enough. The truly shocking part was that he wasn't twisted into bitterness and revenge by loss.

He was stricken with guilt and anguish, however. It showed in the lines that appeared on his face before he turned away again.

"I'm so sorry," she breathed, reaching toward him.

He shrugged off her touch. "There's nothing that can be done. We both know that death is final. Nothing in the past can be reversed."

"No," she agreed, staring at her mottled arm folded across her good one. "You can only learn to live with the consequences. And preserve their memory," she added, feeling as though her chest was scraped hollow like a jack-o'-lantern. "That's what you want to do, isn't it? Achieve what she sacrificed herself for? That's why you'll do anything to bring peace to Bregnovia. You're doing it for her."

"I'm not the only one who lost people, Tiffany. I want it for all of us."

She swallowed, understanding, empathizing, yet feeling very isolated. Her heart ached for him, but for herself, too, because she instinctively wanted to help him. Maybe he was using her, but as he kept demonstrating, his goal was noble. And she loved him too much to refuse him outright when his need and grief were very real.

She loved him.

Staring at the red flecks in the carpet between their feet, she absorbed the bittersweet ache that pulsed through her arteries and settled in her soul. Part of her stood back and mocked herself for having such strong feelings after a mere week and a half of knowing this man. Surely her mother was right and this was a type of Pygmalion infatuation. God knows it was a sexual one.

But when she compared it with what she'd felt for Paulie—exasperated affection and the security of friendship— she knew this was the deeper, more dangerous shade of love. The mature kind that was as threatening as it was fulfilling because it made her needs less important than his. It gave him the power to cripple her with nothing more than his eternal love for another woman.

"I told myself if I couldn't marry Luiza, I wouldn't marry at all." He drained his drink and set it aside, turning to push his hands in his pockets. "Then I met you."

And realized how useful she could be.

"I understand." She fought to keep her brow from pulling.

"Do you? Because I don't. It wasn't a vow of celibacy. I'm not dead. I gave myself permission to have affairs. That ought to be enough. With every other woman it has been."

A strand of something poignant thrummed near her heart. She tried to quell it for the sake of her sanity, trying not to read anything into what he was saying. In a lot of ways what he'd offered her was more than she'd imagined she'd ever find, so she shouldn't be yearning so badly for more.

"I realize you have to look out for your country's best interest, Ryzard. You've been very kind and supportive of me—"

"Oh, shut *up,* Tiffany. Looking out for my country's best interest is how I've been rationalizing your presence in the presidential bed, but even that doesn't work. Do you think I can use you in good conscience after Luiza *died* as a pawn? *Hell, no.* But allowing you to push her out of my heart would be an even greater betrayal."

She could see the tortured struggle in him. He might never love her, not when to do so would mean accepting the debilitating guilt that accompanied it. Who could accept such a deep schism to their soul?

As she absorbed that reality, her breath burned in her lungs like dry smoke.

"But each time you talk of leaving for America, I start thinking about a length of chain about this long." He showed her a space between his hands of two or three feet. "With a cuff here and here." He pointed from his smartwatch to her wrist.

She couldn't help a small smile.

"For such a sophisticated, educated man, you're incredibly uncivilized. You know that, right?" She rubbed the goose bumps off her arms, trying to hide how primitive she was at her core, responding to his caveman talk like some kind of kinky submissive.

"Your parents have every right to be suspicious of me," he allowed drily. "But it's important to me that you know my intentions toward you are not dishonorable."

That's exactly what she had feared after overhearing her mother. It had gutted her. Meeting his gaze was really hard with that specter still haunting her.

"I don't expect you to love me, Ryzard." The words fractured her soul. "But I have to insist on honesty. If you're really just with me because of my father, please say so and I'll—"

"I can't believe I'm going to say this," he cut in impatiently, "but sometimes I wish to hell you'd had other lovers so you would appreciate what we have. *I* do."

"Oh, well, let me just accommodate that right now."

He grabbed her before she'd taken two steps toward the door.

"Gorilla! Brute! You're hurting me," she accused as she found herself bouncing over his shoulder toward the bedroom.

"Honesty, Tiffany," he reminded in a scolding tone. "You just demanded it, and so do I. Lie to me and so help me, I'll spank you. That is not a bluff." He flopped her onto the bed and retreated to slam the bedroom door.

"You scare me," she cried, sitting up. "Not like scared you'll hurt me," she protested with an outstretched hand, trying to forestall the outrage climbing in his expression. "The way you make me feel. I'm terrified you'll stop wanting me. You saw what I was like before you came along. I don't want to be that person again. I don't know how to handle how important you are to me, or how horrible I'll feel when this ends."

The tense line of his shoulders eased. "I can't imagine that happening."

"But I don't know how honorable *my* intentions are. I told you how I feel about living in the public eye. If it's just an affair…"

She trailed off, distracted as he joined her, his big body crowding and overwhelming, sending her onto her back under him with the force of his personality, barely even touching her. She melted in supplication, slave to his authority and the tenderness in his eyes.

"This is more than an affair," he insisted.

That didn't allay any of her misgivings, but she wasn't sure what she wanted him to say. She rather wished she had more experience with relationships herself, but from everything she'd observed, she doubted anyone was truly confident with whatever sorts of relationships they had. It came down to trust, and as much as she wanted to believe in Ryzard, she didn't have much faith in herself.

She touched the pad of her fingertip to his lips, tracing the masculine shape that so entranced her.

"Where do we go from here?" she asked, meaning emotionally, but he took her literally.

"I have quite a few appearances. I would like you to accompany me. Will you?"

Her heart stalled, but refusing meant bringing The End forward to now, and she could already see it would be horribly painful. She wasn't ready for that, so she said the only thing she could.

"Of course."

CHAPTER TEN

DESPITE TIFFANY'S AGREEMENT, despite the unflagging passion between them, she grew less like the cheeky woman he'd come to know and more like the chilly mother he'd met in Zurich.

Of course he was pressing her inexorably into her mother's role. He couldn't help it. The opportunity was too ripe, the timing at hand, and she was damned good at it. She stepped forward with a gracious remark when needed and backed off the rest of the time. No matter what came up or when, she accepted the pull of his attention with equanimity. If she didn't like it, no one could tell, not even him. When he asked, she assured him everything was "Fine."

A sure sign that it wasn't.

But neither of their schedules had room for the type of downtime that had brought them together in the first place. She'd been up for several hours two nights in a row trying to resolve a problem with her firm. Now he'd dragged her to Budapest for an Eastern European conference. A black-tie reception opened the event, and her best makeup couldn't hide the exhaustion around her eyes.

Still she smiled, always ignoring startled reactions to her scars or simply moving past an awkward moment with a calm "Car crash." Then she would distract with a compliment or question, her warm manner disguising the fact she maintained a discreet bubble of distance.

So why was she currently clasping two hands over a stranger's? Her expression was uncharacteristically revealing, not the cool mask she usually wore at these events. The man was older than Ryzard, somewhere in his fifties, but not someone he recognized. Tiffany was sharing deep eye contact with him, and her profile was somber.

He excused himself and crossed over to them, possessive male hackles rising to attention, especially when they both stiffened at his approach and lowered their gazes.

"Ryzard, this is Stanley Griffin, minister of international trade in Canada and my late husband's cousin. Well, cousin to my mother-in-law, Maude."

Despite the legitimate reason for familiarity, he used the introduction to extricate Stanley's hand from Tiffany's grasp.

They briefly chatted about his country's mission to, "Do what we did with the EU here in Eastern Europe." Ryzard expressed his desire to participate, but first he needed recognition so if that message could be conveyed to Canada's prime minister...?

Stanley left with a promise to do so, but made a point to ask Tiffany, "Please stay in touch." Once again, Tiffany had proved her worth to him politically, but her coziness with the man rankled Ryzard for the rest of the evening.

"You seemed very familiar with that Canadian," he said later when they were undressing in the hotel suite. He was tired of being away and wished they were home.

Home. Did she regard his country the way he did? She wasn't happy here in Hungary, despite her expressed desire to see the country and her interest in this city's history. He couldn't be sure she'd been happy in any of the places they'd been recently.

"He was at my wedding. I didn't remember him, to be honest, but he certainly remembered me. He started to tell me how much he loved it when Paulie had spent summers with their family, when the boys were young, and I thought we were both going to—" She clamped her lips together, then pressed a knuckle to her mouth, turning away.

Stricken by her edging toward breakdown, he moved to grasp her shoulders in bracing hands. "Shh. Don't talk about him."

She reacted with a violent twist away from his grip and glared up at him with eyes full of tears and betrayal. "Oh, that's rich. Why can't I talk about my husband? Luiza is right *there* every time we're naked." She poked two fingers into his chest.

Her hostility took him aback, as did the underlying challenge. He bristled, but managed to keep himself from pointing out her scars were an equally indelible reminder that she had had a life before he entered it.

"I didn't say you couldn't talk about him, but it's obviously upsetting you so you should stop," he managed, barely hanging on to a civil tone.

Her jagged laugh abraded his nerves, plucking his aggression responses to even higher alert. "Yeah, well, if that's the criteria, there's a lot of things I should stop doing."

Don't ask, he told himself, but the elephant in the room had grown large enough to put pressure on both of them. A few weeks ago she hadn't had the courage to go to the grocery store in her hometown. Today she was being shoved into a supporting role on the world stage. If she didn't want to do it, she ought to have said so by now, but apparently that was up to him.

"You're not happy in the spotlight. I understand that." He removed his belt and flung it away, angry with himself for turning a blind eye to what was obviously damaging their relationship, but he couldn't undo who he was any more than he was willing to have Luiza's name erased from his chest.

"Stanley said Paulie's mother was always jealous of my

mom because she looked like she had it all, but at least Maude had privacy. All I could think is, *What am I doing? Why am I here?*" She lifted helpless hands.

"Tiffany, you're good at this," he began.

"I'm good at sex. Should I do that with every man who asks?" she snarled back.

He recoiled, shocked by her vehemence and scored by a remark that made it sound as if she only tolerated sleeping with him. "As I said—" The words ground from between his clenched teeth. "You shouldn't do anything that fails to give you some level of enjoyment."

Her fierce expression flickered toward remorse, before she collapsed in a chair, elbows on her knees, head in hands, shoulders heavy with defeat. "I'm sorry. I know better than to have this fight. It accomplishes nothing because at the end of the day, you still need me beside you."

"I *want* you beside me, Tiffany. I don't need you. If you're feeling used then you know my feelings on that. I'll achieve my two-thirds votes with or without you."

She lifted her head out of her hands to stare at him, face like a mask, half of it tortoiseshell reds, the other side white. Slowly her flat gaze moved to the floor while her hands twisted together. She forced herself to sit upright, but her shoulders remained bowed.

"That certainly tells me where I stand."

The ice maiden was back, causing cold fire to lick behind his heart, leaving streaks of dead, black tissue.

"I'm saying you don't have to participate if you don't want to. We can still be together. It doesn't have to change anything," he said rather desperately, sensing things slipping away without any chance to control it.

"It changes everything, Ryzard! What am I going to do? Sit in your presidential castle waiting for you to come home? *There's* a departure from turning into my mother," she said with a caustic laugh. "What else could I do? Follow you around but never be seen? That would be living as a recluse again. If you—" She bent her head to stare at her pale knuckles, but he saw the pull in her brow of deep struggle. "If we loved each other, it would be different."

He couldn't help his stark inhale of aversion. Marriage he might rationalize. Pulling his heart from the grave where he'd buried it next to Luiza was impossible. There, at least, it was safe from another blow of great loss.

Silence coated the room in a thick fog for a long minute. Tiffany was the first to move, swiping at her cheek before speaking haltingly.

"I thought my life was over, that I'd never be able to have a husband and family. I even reconciled myself to it and figured out how to fill my life with other things. I could live unmarried and childless with you, Ryzard. But you're the one who made me believe I shouldn't sell myself short. If someone could love me, if I have a soul mate out there, I shouldn't settle for anything less than finding him."

He clenched his hands into fists, trying to withstand a pain so great it threatened to rend him apart. She *did* deserve to be loved. He couldn't keep her here to serve his passion while he withheld parts of himself. It would wear on her self-esteem. If he wasn't capable of giving her all of himself, he had to let her go.

But the agony was so great he wanted to scream.

The weariness and misery in her eyes when she lifted them to meet his gaze was more than he could bear though.

"It's time for me to go home," she said gently.

He nodded once, jerkily, incapable of any other response. His throat was blocked by a thick knot of anguish, the rest of him caved in on itself so his skin felt like a thin shell, ready to crack and turn to powder.

"I'll go make the arrangements," her voice thinned over the last word as she stood and rushed from the room.

She didn't return.

When he couldn't stand it any longer, he went looking for her and came up against a locked door. He could hear her sobbing inside the bedroom, but he didn't knock. He silently railed at her for shutting him out, but the truth was, he was close to tears himself. Drowning himself in a bottle of vodka looked like a really good idea.

Taking one to his room, he sat on the bed then left it untouched on the nightstand as he stayed awake through the long, dark night, willing Tiffany to come to him.

CHAPTER ELEVEN

BARBARA HOLBROOK WANTED to know exactly what had happened.

"Mom," Tiffany protested, feeling cornered in her room, jet-lagged and wondering how she still had a doll propped on the pillows of her made bed. It was an antique, granted, but seriously. "I'm about ten years too late for having my heart broken by my first crush. That's all it was."

That's what she kept telling herself anyway. She sure as heck didn't want to deconstruct everything that had happened with Ryzard. It was too painful.

But she missed him. Sleeping alone sucked and stalking him on the web only made her heart ache. Or laugh aloud.

Mrs. Davis and I remain on excellent terms. Print something negative about her at your own peril, she read over breakfast one Saturday morning and got herself goggled at by her entire family for her outburst.

"What," she hedged, amusement fading. "It's funny," she insisted after reading it to them. She wanted to kiss his austere image, feeling as though he was flirting with her from far, far away. He'd been so contained that last night, so willing to let her go without a fight. That had made her feel insignificant, but reading that they remained "on excellent terms" bolstered her.

"You'll be seeing him again, then?" her father asked, sipping his coffee.

"Why? Does sleeping with him help your approval rating?"

"Tiffany," her mother gasped.

Christian sent her a hard look. "Come on, Tiff."

Setting her cup into its saucer like a gavel announcing a judge's decision, Tiffany said, "That was out of line. I apologize. But I'm tired of being a bug under a microscope. It's time I went into the office."

"You've been in there every day since you came home," her mother said with confusion.

"Not my office here, Mom. The real office. In the city."

"What? When?" Chris asked swiftly. "I can't drive you for a week at least. I told you I'm working from here until I get that design done, so I'm not interrupted."

"And I have to be in Washington," her father said with apology.

"I have an appointment in New York at the end of the month, darling," her mother offered. "You can come in for the day with me, but are you sure you're ready?"

She wished she'd had her tablet set to record. Ryzard would shake his head at this display and probably claim this coddling was the reason she was such a spoiled brat. She suspected he'd also remind her how lucky she was to be so loved.

Misty emotion washed over her in a flood of gratitude for the family she had and an ache of longing for the man she didn't.

"You guys are awesome. I love you," she said, meeting each pair of eyes in turn to let her sincerity sink in. She silently thanked Ryzard as she did it, finally able to see herself as a whole, independent adult because he had treated her as one. "But it's time for me to be a grown-up. I'll drive myself to New York and stay in the company flat until I find my own place."

Her mother's gasp and near Victorian collapse didn't

sway her. On Monday she walked through the glass doors of Davis and Holbrook, palms clammy and half her face hidden behind giant sunglasses. By Thursday the worst of the buzzing and staring was behind her. Friday morning she was interrupted by a delivery of flowers.

"Wow," she couldn't help saying, stunned by the bouquet arranged to look like a culmination of fireworks. Her heart began to gallop in her chest. "Who is that from?"

"I couldn't say, ma'am." The uniformed man tapped the subtle *Q Virtus* crest on his shirt pocket. "I work for their concierge service. All I get is a pickup and delivery address."

"Oh, um, would it be from *Q Virtus* itself, then?" That was disappointing. And made the significance of portraying fireworks a little creepy.

"There's usually a 'compliments of Zeus' card if it is. Without one, I'd guess it's from one of their members, but I really couldn't say. I'm not privy to much that goes on there. *You* could be a member for all I know," he added with a shrug.

"I imagine there are members who don't know they belong," she murmured ironically, thanking him with a generous tip, then burying her face in the perfume of the bouquet. She wanted to gather the fragrant leaves and butter-soft petals into herself, trying to feel closer to Ryzard.

How could he be this sweet, this pleased by her stepping out of her comfort zone and taking control of her life, and not love her a little?

Luiza, she thought with a pang. She could never compete with a woman who had shown such a level of bravery.

Taking a page from Ryzard's book, she had *Q Virtus* arrange a nice lunch when her mother came to visit at the end of the month. Being scrupulously efficient, they located it in a penthouse that fit exactly what Tiffany was looking for as a new home. The decor was a bit too colorless for her taste. It needed a stained glass umbrella to jazz it up, but the floor plan and views were astonishing.

Her mother pronounced it excellent for entertaining, which only made Tiffany think of holding court with Ryzard and miss him all over again.

She sat across from her mother in tall wingbacks at a circle of white marble facing a floor-to-ceiling view of Central Park, sipping from crystal water goblets with brushed gold trim, thinking she'd rather be staring at that heart-wrenching statue if it put her back in his proximity.

"This isn't at all how I imagined things turning out for you," her mother murmured.

She seemed surprised that the words had escaped her and glanced toward the kitchen, where the noise and staff were well contained beyond a small service pantry.

Tiffany set down her glass and linked her fingers together, subtly bracing for reaction as she admitted, "I think it might have come to this eventually. I didn't love Paulie. Not in a way that would have kept us together forever."

"I know," Barbara sighed.

"You did?"

Her mother's perfectly coiffed head tilted in acknowledgement. "Not until you started up with that Bregnovian fellow, but once I saw the lengths you were willing to go for him, I realized you and Paulie never stood a chance. I should have seen it from the outset, but it would have been so convenient, Tiffany."

She sputtered a laugh at that. "Yeah, well, the situation with Ryzard was more convenience on his part. You were right about that much." Deep angst threatened to rise up and squeeze her in its clawed grip.

"Is that true? He seemed so protective of you. Still does."

"I think that's his nature," Tiffany said shakily, finding it really hard to hold on to her control. "He was so supportive, made me feel so good about myself, but when it came down to it he said he didn't need me or my connections. He—" Her voice broke, but she had to say it aloud so she could get over it and move on. "He doesn't love me."

"But you love him."

Through blurred eyes, Tiffany saw her mother's hand cover her own. The gesture was bittersweet and made her think of all the times her mother had held her hand through her recovery. Through her whole life. She was the wrong person to be mad at.

"I shouldn't have pushed you away so much lately," she husked.

"Shush. Your brother did it when he was eleven. I've been lucky enough to keep you close this long. I'm just glad I can be here for you when you need me."

"Are you going to tell me there's plenty more fish in the sea?"

"I'd like to, but there are so few worth reeling in," her mother bemoaned, making Tiffany chortle past her tears. "It's so good to see you smiling again," her mother added with her own misty smile.

She didn't know how often Tiffany cried. How she combed for news and photos of Ryzard, how she quietly kept tally of the countries recognizing him. She was doing exactly that one afternoon before going into a meeting, getting her fix to get her through one more day without him, when she came across a horrifying update.

Coal Mine Explosion in Northern Bregnovia, Dozens Unaccounted For, one hour ago.

Leaping to her feet, she shouted for her assistant.

Even though sabotage was not suspected, it was war conditions all over again. Ryzard could hardly bear it, but quick response on the recovery effort was critical. There was no time to ask the fates why his country should suffer this way. No way to reassure his people that they could live without fear. There were only feet on the ground, hands digging into the rubble, people trying to save people into the night.

Dark was receding, exhaustion setting in and spirits low when a throaty drone began climbing on the air. The latest batch of survivors, many badly burned, had just left on what aircraft he'd been able to muster on short notice. They hadn't had time to drop and be back so soon. That didn't bode well.

Squinting into the silver horizon, he saw what looked like an invasion, and his heart stopped. Then the hospital crosses on the underbellies of three of the helicopters became visible and he relaxed. Someone asked if the Red Cross was finally here. He had no idea. His phone was charging in the one small shack that had a power generator for electricity.

Jerking his chin at someone to greet and direct them, he threw himself back into the work at hand.

Sixteen hours later, he was knee-deep in rubble, numb and almost asleep on his feet, losing the light, when his eye—and half-dead libido—was caught unexpectedly by a pair of skintight jeans tucked into knee-high black boots. A blond ponytail swung against the back of a black leather jacket as the woman nodded at whomever she was speaking to.

He was seeing things. He clambered across to her, swaying on his feet as he pulled her around by a rather despondent grip on her arm, distantly surprised to catch at a solid person and still not believing his eyes, even when he saw the familiar patch of color on the side of her face.

"You're real," he said dumbly.

She smiled tenderly and set a hand against his cheek. Her touch was surprisingly warm, making him aware how cold he was. How utterly empty and frozen he'd been for weeks.

"All I could think was that no country would be equipped for this many burn injuries. We have a triage set up. I hope you don't mind, but I'm sending the victims with their families to whoever can take them."

He couldn't speak, could only string clumsy arms around her and drag her into him. Closing his eyes, he drank in the sweet, familiar scent of her hair.

Tiffany ran soothing hands over him, feeling the chill on his skin beneath his shirt, trying to ease the shudders rippling through his muscles. He was heavy, leaning into her, beyond exhausted.

"Come with me," she urged, dragging him stumbling across the trampled yard to the tent where cots and coffee were on hand for the rescuers.

His arm was deadweight across her shoulders. When he sat, he pulled her into his lap.

"You need to sleep," she insisted as she tried to extricate herself.

He said something in Bregnovian, voice jagged and broken. He snugged her closer, his hold unbreakable.

Not that she really wanted to get away. It felt so good to be near him. He was grimy and sweaty, but he was Ryzard. She blinked damp eyes where he was keeping her face trapped against his chest, surrounded in his personal scent.

"You need to lie down, Ryzard. You're not even speaking English."

He brought her with him so the cot groaned beneath them. When she tried to rise, he threw a pinning leg across her and tangled his fingers in her hair. "Don't leave," he murmured and the lights went out. He became a lead blanket upon her.

Since she was jet-lagged and had been on her feet for hours, she relaxed and dozed until activity around them woke her. Then she managed to climb free of his tentacle-like hold and carry on with the rescue effort. The trapped miners had been reached and the final victims would need transport.

* * *

Ryzard woke thinking he'd dreamed her, but the jacket draped across his chest told him he wasn't crazy. She was here, somewhere.

Coffee in one hand, jacket in his other, he went in search and found her trying to comfort an anxious wife as an injured miner was packaged into a helicopter. The woman clutched a baby and had a redheaded boy by the hand, and Tiffany held a matching toddler on her hip.

"Oh, Ryzard," she said when he draped her jacket over her shoulders, "Please tell her I'm sure her husband will live. The burns are bad, but they didn't find internal injuries. I've lost my translator and she's so upset."

Together they reassured the woman and made arrangements for her to catch up with her husband at the burn unit in Paris.

Calm settled as everyone was accounted for. There was a longer journey ahead to bring the mine back into operation, but the immediate crisis was over. Tiffany stifled a yawn as she thanked people and gave them final directions for breaking down the field hospital they'd erected.

"I can't thank you enough for this," Ryzard said.

"When you're part of a club, you pitch in to help your fellow members when they need it, right?"

She was being her cheeky self, but he wasn't in a frame of mind to take this gesture so lightheartedly.

"I'm being sincere, Tiffany. I hope your motives were not that superficial."

She sobered. "I told you last night that this struck close to home for me. But I don't suppose you remember, being pretty much sleepwalking at the time."

Was it only empathy for fellow burn victims that had brought her here? He flinched, wondering where he got off imagining she could have deeper feelings for him when he'd pushed her from his life the way he had.

"Hey, Tiff," some flyboy called across. "You catching a lift in my bird or...?"

"Oh, um—"

Ryzard cut her off before she could answer. "You'll come to Gizela with me."

"Will I," she said in the tone she used when she thought he was being arrogant, but he only cared that she acquiesced. He did *not* care for the way she hugged the pilot and kissed his cheek, thanking him for his help.

Ryzard lifted his brows in query when she turned from her goodbye.

"He grew up with Paulie and my brother. I've known him forever," she defended. "We needed pilots so I called him."

It was petty and ungrateful to think, we didn't need them *that* badly, but he was still short on sleep and deeply deprived of her. His willingness to share her, especially when he was so uncertain how long he'd have her, was nil.

His own transport arrived. They fell asleep against each other in the back of the 4x4 for the jostling four-hour drive back to Gizela.

The palace looked better than ever, Tiffany noted when she woke in front of it. Its exterior was no longer pockmarked by bullet holes and the broken stones were gone, giving the grounds a sense of openness and welcome. Inside, she went straight up the stairs next to Ryzard, both anxious for a shower. They parted at the top and she went to her room, where, he had assured her, everything she'd left was still there.

She wasn't sure what it meant. A dozen times she'd thought about asking for the items to be shipped, but she'd been afraid that contacting him would be the first step toward falling back down the rabbit hole into his world. Or it would have been final closure, something she hadn't been ready for. Had he felt the same? Because he could have had the things shipped to her at any time.

The not knowing hung like a veil over the situation, making her wonder if she was being silly and desperate when she dressed for his flag salutation, or respectful and supportive. He wouldn't have brought her here if he didn't want her here, she told herself, but she faltered when they met at the top of the stairs.

He wore his white shirt, black suit and presidential sash. His jaw was freshly shaved and sharply defined by tension as he took in her houndstooth skirt and matching wool jacket. "You don't have to," he said for the second time.

She almost took him at his word, almost let herself believe that he only wanted her, didn't need her, but his eyes gave him away. They weren't flat green. They burned gold. As if he was taking in treasure. As if she said she wasn't ready, he would wait until she was.

"I want to," she assured him, wondering if she was being an imaginative fool. Why would she want to do this? Pride of place, she guessed. It made her feel good to be with him no matter what he was doing. She admired him as a man and took great joy in watching him rise to his position.

Outside, it was blustery and tasting of an early-fall storm with spits of rain in the gusting wind. Leaves chased across grass and their clothes rippled as they walked to the pole. The flag snapped its green and blue stripes as he made his pledge and saluted it.

A burst of applause made them both turn to the crowd gathered at the gate. It was a deeper gathering than Tiffany had seen any other time. Hundreds maybe. A fresh rush of pride welled in her.

"Your predecessor wouldn't have cut up his hands freeing trapped miners," she said, picking up his scabbed hand. It was so roughened and abused, she instinctively lifted it to her lips.

The cheering swelled, making her pull back from touching him. "Sorry. That was dumb."

"No, they liked it. They're here for you as much as me. They know what you did for us." He faced the crowd and indicated her with a sweep of his hand and a bow of his head.

His people reacted with incendiary passion, waving flags and holding up children.

"They're thanking you, Tiffany." He lifted her hand to his own lips, and another roar went up.

They stood there a long time, hands linked, waving at the crowd. No one walked away. They waited for her and Ryzard to go in first.

"Are you crying?" he asked as they entered the big drawing room. It was such a stunning room with its gorgeous nineteenth-century furniture and view overlooking the sea, but she still wasn't comfortable in it.

Averting her gaze from Luiza's portrait, she swiped at her cheeks. "That was very moving. I didn't expect it. I had the impression they thought of me as an interloper." Now she couldn't help straying a glance at Luiza, as if the woman might be eavesdropping.

For a long moment he didn't say anything, only looked at the portrait with the same tortured expression she'd seen on him before, when his feelings for Luiza were too close to the surface.

She looked away, respecting his need for time to pull himself together, but taking a hit of despair over it, too.

"It's my fault you felt that way," he said in a low, grave voice. "But please try to understand what she meant to me. Luiza made me see that Bregnovia is my home. That if I fought for it and made it ours, *mine*—" he set his fist over the place where her name was inked forever "—I would always belong here. That was deeply meaningful after so many years of being rootless and displaced."

She nodded, unable to speak because she did understand and felt for him.

"I needed her love after losing my parents. I would have shut down otherwise. Become an instrument of war."

Instead of a leader who had retained his humanity. It was one of the qualities she admired most in him, so she could hardly begrudge the woman who'd kept his heart intact through the horrors of battle and loss.

"When I lost her, I couldn't let myself become embittered and filled with hatred. It would have gone against everything she helped me become, but I couldn't face another loss like it. The vulnerability of loving again, knowing the emotional pain of grief if something were to happen... It terrifies me, Tiffany."

He said it so plainly, never faltering even when he was exposing his deepest fear.

She wanted to look to the ceiling to contain the tears gathering to sting her eyes. It killed her to hear that he couldn't give up his heart, but she couldn't look away from him.

"It's okay. I admire her, too," she managed. Her voice scraped her throat with emotion, but she was being sincere. "I wish I'd met her. She had amazing willpower. I wouldn't have had the guts to do what she did."

"Guts." The harsh sound he made was halfway between a laugh and a choke of deep anguish. "Luiza had ideals. Now she is our martyr and a symbol of our sacrifice and loss. I would do her a disservice to forget or dismiss that, but it doesn't make you an interloper for living where she died, Tiffany. She had a vision. When I look at you, I see reality. Our reality. Scarred by tragedy, but so beautiful. So strong and determined to carry on."

His tender look of regard had its usual effect of striking like an unexpected punch into her solar plexus, making her breath rush out. She had to cover her lips to still them from trembling.

"I don't like comparing you. It's disrespectful to both of you, but you're right. You and Luiza are very different. You wouldn't have killed yourself. Given the same situation, you would fight with everything in you to stay alive until I came for you, no matter what happened. That's who you are. Your courage astounds me."

He ran his hand down his face only to reveal an expression of profound regret.

"When I sent you away, all I could think was that I didn't want to risk the pain of loss again. And did you crawl back in your cave even though I'd hurt you? No. You went on with your life without me, and I was so hurt and so proud at the same time."

She lowered her head, touched beyond measure, and saw a teardrop land on the hardwood. She swiped at her numb cheek, finding it wet. "Thank you for the flowers."

"The flowers were an apology. You made me feel like a coward, refusing to embrace love when it's as precious as life. I wanted to come to you and to hell with your Customs and Immigration, but I had to finish my obligation to Luiza first. I've done that. Official announcements will be made later in the week. I have the votes I need."

"Oh, Ryzard, that's wonderful!" She was elated for him, but still reeling from his mention of embracing love. Did that mean…? She searched his inscrutable expression.

"After the last few days, this country needs good news." He sighed and rocked back on his heels, regarding her. "It also means the worst is over for a time when it comes to state functions. I won't run in the next election. Could you live with two more years of being in the public eye, knowing it would be temporary?"

"What?" Her nails cut into her palms as she tried to stay grounded, not leaping too high on what he was saying. Not reading too deep. Definitely not wanting to hold him back in any way. "Ryzard, you *are* Bregnovia. It's barely on its feet. You can't hand it over to someone else so soon. I couldn't live with myself if all this stability you've fought for crumbled."

"I don't want to wait that long to marry you, *draga*. I ache every night and barely get through my days. I need you."

"You do?" Her voice hitched and stayed awfully small, but the world around her seemed to expand in one pulse beat, stealing the oxygen and filling the air with sparks. "You really want to marry me? *Me?*"

"*You*. Not the daughter of the next American president, not Davis and Holbrook, not the woman who charms heads of state without even trying. You."

"Because you love me?" she hazarded, curling her toes and pulling her elbows in, bracing for the worst.

"Because we love each other."

His tender gaze held hers, gently demanding she give up her heart to him. She did, easily.

"If I hadn't been trained from birth to pretend everything was fine no matter how miserable I was, I couldn't have got through these last weeks. I love you so much, Ryzard, and I hated myself for not letting my love be enough to keep us together."

"I shouldn't have made you feel like it was all up to you," he said, coming across to draw her into him. With his lips pressed to her forehead, he added, "I will never hold back from you again. I thought I was being noble, letting you find the man who would love you like no other could, but that man is me. I love you with every breath in me, Tiffany. A different man loved Luiza. This one is yours."

She relaxed her forehead against his nuzzling lips, touched to her soul. Fulfilled. Hopeful. *Happy*.

He traced a soft kiss along the raised line of her scar,

following it down to the corner of her eye and across her cheek until he was almost at her mouth.

"We should take this upstairs," she said against his lips. "I have a feeling it won't stay PG rated for long."

He quirked a rueful grin and led her upstairs. In his bedroom, he took a moment to lift the snapshot from his bedside table and walk it into his sitting room.

When he returned he found her seated on the bed, hands tucked in her lap.

"We have to talk about one more thing before we go any further," she said.

"What's that?" he queried.

"Children."

"At least two. I want them to have each other if something happens to us," he affirmed.

"I was going to say six, but okay. Coward."

"Ambitious," he remarked in a drawl. "I can keep up if you can." His smile was a slow dawn of masculine heat that twitched with amusement. "I've missed you, Tiffany. You make me laugh."

She threw herself into his arms.

EPILOGUE

THE MILKY WAY stretched from one edge of the horizon to the other, diffusing into more stars against Zanzibar's indigo sky than Tiffany had ever seen in her life. If Ryzard hadn't kept her pressed firmly against his side as he steered them down the jetty toward the island bar, she likely would have stumbled into the lagoon.

"What the hell are you up to?"

"I know, I'm sorry, but I've never seen anything like—wait, what?" She realized Ryzard had been talking to a man in a mask who'd just passed them on the jetty. She glanced back the way they'd come to see the member break off his lip-lock with a *petite q* and hurry her toward the interior of the club.

"Who was that?"

"A friend. One who knows better than to play with Zeus's toys." He dragged his puzzled gaze to her expectant one. With a low sigh, he bent to whisper, "His name is Nic." Straightening, he added, "Don't ask me to say more than that. Even though you're my wife, I still have an obligation to respect other members' privacy."

She grinned, pleased more by her title of "wife" than anything else.

The DJ's electronica pulsed louder as they finished their walk into the open-air bar. *Q Virtus* members and *petite q's* danced and jumped to the beat, making the wooden floor bounce.

Tiffany refused a drink offered by a passing *petite q,* but Ryzard drew her to a side bar. "Iced coconut. Nonalcoholic," he said.

Her condition wasn't official, especially since they'd been married only a day, but they'd stopped using protection weeks ago. She was pretty sure, and they were both so quietly, ferociously happy it was criminal.

The server tilted his array of cones for her to peruse. They were stunning, not merely shaved and frozen coconut with a splash of color, but intricately decorated works of art in more shades, flavors and hues than the stars above them.

Tiffany almost picked the one that looked like a bouquet of sweet peas, but maybe the mandala was prettier. The paisley?

"It just hit me," Ryzard said in a tone of discovery. "It was never about the taffy apple being better optics. You couldn't decide what color candy floss you wanted."

Grinning, she admitted, "You caught me."

"I'm convinced it's the other way around, *draga,*" he retorted.

She laughed in delight, but contradicted, "I distinctly remember a kidnapping on the high seas."

"I remember fireworks," he said with a smoky look from behind his mask. "Choose something or we'll miss these ones."

Face warm with pleasure behind her own mask, she took two cones and gave him one, leaning her weight into him as he hooked his arm across her shoulders and steered her toward the rail overlooking the Indian Ocean.

"I see them every night, you know. Fireworks. 'Cause I'm spoiled."

"You are," he agreed, leaning down to bite at her cone before he offered his. "So am I."

"Mmm. We're in the right place for the privileged, aren't we?" she mused, licking clove-and-orange-flavored coconut from her lips.

He stopped and turned her so they held each other in a way that felt perfect and familiar and right. "As long as I'm with you, I'm exactly where I belong."

* * * * *

If you enjoyed this book,
look out for the next instalment of
THE 21ST CENTURY GENTLEMAN'S CLUB:
THE ULTIMATE REVENGE
by Victoria Parker
Coming next month!

COMING NEXT MONTH FROM
HARLEQUIN *Presents*

Available August 19, 2014

#3265 TYCOON'S TEMPTATION
The Chatsfield
by Trish Morey

Franco Chatsfield must secure a partnership with Holly Purman's vineyard, the family business she's devoted her whole life to. She'll give Franco six weeks to prove himself, but working together sends their senses reeling—one taste just isn't enough!

#3266 THE HOUSEKEEPER'S AWAKENING
At His Service
by Sharon Kendrick

Injured playboy Luis Martinez is sick of nurses and demands his sweet, innocent housekeeper Carly Conner massage him back to health! Whisked away to the south of France, how long will she be able to deny tantalizing tension between them?

#3267 MORE PRECIOUS THAN A CROWN
by Carol Marinelli

Prince Zahid, heir to the Kingdom of Ishla, once walked away from the fire blazing in Trinity Foster's eyes. Now, after one earth-shattering night, it's revealed that Trinity needs Zahid's protection. She's strictly forbidden, but walking away again may prove impossible....

#3268 CAPTURED BY THE SHEIKH
Rivals to the Crown of Kadar
by Kate Hewitt

Sheikh Khalil's first step to reclaiming his crown is to kidnap his rival's bride-to-be, Elena Karras. Expecting a cold, convenient marriage, this virgin queen is instead carried into the sands, where she discovers an unexpected desire for her sinfully sexy captor!

HPCNM0814RA

#3269 A NIGHT IN THE PRINCE'S BED
by Chantelle Shaw

For deaf theater actress Mina Hart, one night with a gorgeous stranger turns into headline news when he's revealed as Prince Aksel of Storvhal. Trapped in icy Scandinavia, can Mina rely on her senses to read this intensely private prince?

#3270 DAMASO CLAIMS HIS HEIR
One Night With Consequences
by Annie West

The virtue behind Princess Marisa's scandalous reputation touched a place in Damaso Pires that he'd thought long destroyed. But their brief affair becomes permanent when Marisa reveals she's pregnant.... There's only one way for Damaso to claim his heir—marriage!

#3271 CHANGING CONSTANTINOU'S GAME
by Jennifer Hayward

All bets are off when reporter Isabel Peters is dropped into Alexios Constantinou's lap during a hellish elevator ride—especially when he discovers that her next story is *him!* With everything at stake, he'll need a whole new game plan....

#3272 THE ULTIMATE REVENGE
The 21st Century Gentleman's Club
by Victoria Parker

Nicandro Santos is determined to bring down the ultra-prestigious *Q Virtus* gentleman's club. But with his enemy's daughter, Olympia Merisi, now in charge, the battle lines between this pair soon blur, and they risk entering more *sensual* territory....

YOU CAN FIND MORE INFORMATION ON UPCOMING HARLEQUIN° TITLES, FREE EXCERPTS AND MORE AT WWW.HARLEQUIN.COM.

HPCNM0814RB

REQUEST YOUR
FREE BOOKS!

2 FREE NOVELS PLUS
2 FREE GIFTS!

YES! Please send me 2 FREE Harlequin Presents® novels and my 2 FREE gifts (gifts are worth about $10). After receiving them, if I don't wish to receive any more books, I can return the shipping statement marked "cancel." If I don't cancel, I will receive 6 brand-new novels every month and be billed just $4.30 per book in the U.S. or $4.99 per book in Canada. That's a saving of at least 14% off the cover price! It's quite a bargain! Shipping and handling is just 50¢ per book in the U.S. and 75¢ per book in Canada.* I understand that accepting the 2 free books and gifts places me under no obligation to buy anything. I can always return a shipment and cancel at any time. Even if I never buy another book, the two free books and gifts are mine to keep forever.

106/306 HDN FVRK

Name _____ (PLEASE PRINT)

Address _____ Apt. #

City _____ State/Prov. _____ Zip/Postal Code

Signature (if under 18, a parent or guardian must sign)

Mail to the **Harlequin® Reader Service:**
IN U.S.A.: P.O. Box 1867, Buffalo, NY 14240-1867
IN CANADA: P.O. Box 609, Fort Erie, Ontario L2A 5X3

Are you a current subscriber to Harlequin Presents books
and want to receive the larger-print edition?
Call 1-800-873-8635 or visit www.ReaderService.com.

* Terms and prices subject to change without notice. Prices do not include applicable taxes. Sales tax applicable in N.Y. Canadian residents will be charged applicable taxes. Offer not valid in Quebec. This offer is limited to one order per household. Not valid for current subscribers to Harlequin Presents books. All orders subject to credit approval. Credit or debit balances in a customer's account(s) may be offset by any other outstanding balance owed by or to the customer. Please allow 4 to 6 weeks for delivery. Offer available while quantities last.

Your Privacy—The Harlequin® Reader Service is committed to protecting your privacy. Our Privacy Policy is available online at www.ReaderService.com or upon request from the Harlequin Reader Service.

We make a portion of our mailing list available to reputable third parties that offer products we believe may interest you. If you prefer that we not exchange your name with third parties, or if you wish to clarify or modify your communication preferences, please visit us at www.ReaderService.com/consumerschoice or write to us at Harlequin Reader Service Preference Service, P.O. Box 9062, Buffalo, NY 14269. Include your complete name and address.

HP13